CHRISTOPHER BURNS

Christopher Burns was born in 1944 in the small town of Egremont in Cumbria. He has had three novels published: SNAKEWRIST, THE FLINT BED (which was short-listed for the Whitbread Novel of the Year award in 1989), and THE CONDITION OF ICE, which will also be published by Sceptre. His stories have appeared in the *London Review of Books, London Magazine* and the *Critical Quarterly*, in Heinemann's *Best Short Stories* in 1986 and 1988, and in the collection ABOUT THE BODY, published in 1988 and also available from Sceptre. He is married with two sons and lives in Cumbria.

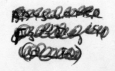

Christopher Burns

THE FLINT BED

First published in Great Britain in 1989 by Martin Secker & Warburg Ltd.

Sceptre edition 1991

Sceptre is an imprint of Hodder and Stoughton Paperbacks, a division of Hodder and Stoughton Ltd.

British Library C.I.P.

Burns, Christopher, *1944–*
   The flint bed.
   I. Title
   823'.914[F]

ISBN 0-340-53042-1

Printed and bound in Great Britain for Hodder and Stoughton Paperbacks, a division of Hodder and Stoughton Ltd., Mill Road, Dunton Green, Sevenoaks, Kent TN13 2YA. (Editorial Office: 47 Bedford Square, London WC1B 3DP) by Clays Ltd., St Ives plc.

For Mike O'Pray and Jill McGreal

1

DURING THE NIGHT A FOX HUNTED THE DUNES. I heard it bark near the cottage, and knew that it would be on its way to the nesting sites. It was not an unusual event and, as I lay in bed in the darkness, I had little thought but for the gulls taken from their roosts and slaughtered. Only after Croft's visit did such a raid assume a greater significance, and every journey through the reserve suggest a history. Now I spend my time reliving events and examining the detail of every conversation that we had. Often, having given me no rest during the day, Croft and his girl return to me at night and trouble my dreams.

That morning the wind could be heard in the chimney and I could smell the sea across my narrow strip of land. The telegraph-pole moaned at the side of the cottage and shrub thrashed along the railway embankment. The mail-van left me a circular, a wildlife magazine and a letter from my daughter. I crumpled the circular and dropped it on the fire, left Jessica's letter unopened on the table, and read articles in the magazine while I drank my tea.

The telephone rang.

'Morning, Reverend Fretwell.'

I sighed. 'That wore thin a long time ago, Celia.'

Her voice was cheerful but with a hint of pushiness. 'Don't you believe it; some people round here still think of you as their vicar.'

'You mean they think I'm in hiding,' I said drily, 'waiting for the call to reclaim my rightful parish?'

Her laugh was made tinny by the earpiece. 'I like that.'

'It's off the record, if you're thinking of using it. And you know I wished the new man all the best. But I don't think you rang just to hear a droll remark.'

'How right you are, Maurice.'

'The article, is it? I've got it here. I would have given it to the postman if I'd thought.'

'Good,' she said, but there was a flatness in the way that she said it, as if she did not wish to talk about the piece she had asked me to write. I sympathised with that; she had never expressed any real interest in archaeology or prehistory. But I had promised to deliver it a week ago, and I felt mildly guilty that I had not done so.

'Is that all right?' I asked. Celia and I had known each other for several years; possibly we were even

2

friends. But I was still suspicious that I might say something in an unguarded moment that she would wish me to follow up. I was tired of controversy; I merely wanted my solitude, my books, my land.

'If you're happy with it, I can pick it up. If you want.'

'It's a long way to drive just for that. What's happened? Are you wanting my opinion on something I should know about?'

'Maurice, I've always been above board with you. People in my position can't afford to be too devious. Besides, I'm too long in the tooth to be ambitious in that foot-in-the-door sense. But you're right, there is something I'd like your opinion on.'

'Is this official or unofficial?'

'Strictly between you and me, for the moment. I'll buy you an early lunch, if you like. On the *News*.'

'All right,' I said, unenthusiastically.

'Besides,' she confessed, 'I could do with a couple of hours away from this. You know what I mean – all this endless processing of ephemera. There's no end to the pettiness of the information I have to deal with.'

I clicked my tongue in mock disapproval. 'You should be loyal to your readership, Celia.'

As soon as I said it there was a slight pause, and I knew that she had formulated a response but not made it. Many of the people she had talked to must have accused me of disloyalty.

'I want to see you about a letter,' she went on, 'from a man called Luciano Croft. The name's not familiar?'

'Should it be? Does he know me?'

'Don't worry, you're not mentioned in it. And he won't know you. But you may be able to help him.'

'Does he want to visit the reserve? If not, then my helping days are over. Everyone knows that.'

'We'll see. I'll call just before twelve. All right?'

I agreed and went back to my magazine. It was half an hour before I picked up Jessica's letter. As usual, it was an air letter, eggshell blue, thinner and lighter than a wafer. When I turned it over I saw that her address was still the same and that she had inked into one corner her usual Hindu good-luck sign. Often I had thought of burning Jessica's letters without even reading them. Although apparently callous, this might have been the best thing to do. I gained a certain amount of self-righteous pleasure in thinking of my life ending here in this lonely cottage, with no one near me and no one to hear my last words or witness my moment of extinction. I certainly did not want Jessica to fly from half a world away and fill my final hours with lame mystical panaceas.

But I could never do it. Instead I played a strange game with her letters, and always delayed reading them by pretending there were more important things

4

THE FLINT BED

to do. Usually, that was true. I had often gone for
hours, or even a full day, before I opened one. That
morning, once I had read articles about hedgehogs
and puffins and Sites of Special Scientific Interest, I
could think of no further reason to delay, although
I did consider going straight out onto the reserve to
see what damage the fox had done.

I picked up the envelope, which still smelled of
the alien, spicy perfume she must have sprinkled
on it, and sliced it with a knife so that it could be
unfolded. *Dear Dad*, she began. In her twenties she
sometimes called me Father, or, after the children
were born, Grandfather. Often, as if embarrassed
by her relationship to me, she called me nothing at
all. Now, at the age of thirty-eight, she had started
to call me Dad again. I did not believe that it was
cynicism which made me think that this had something to do with all those Americans out there, all
those wandering souls who sent back letters to folks
in Idaho and Montana and New York City.

First of all there was a description of the morning
on which she had written the letter. Many of her
letters were crammed with description, which I usually skipped. There were whole sentences about the
green parrots with bright blue tails that flew round
their house and came in the door looking for food.
Jessica felt good that morning. Yesterday she had felt
bad and Rick, her second husband, had said she was

5

at the bottom of a trough, biorhythmically speaking. She just couldn't rid herself of frustration at the state of the world. Rick had persuaded her to see Teacher, and she wasn't due to see him, but she crossed the fields and asked for a special favour. He said yes, he'd talk to her, but she did most of the talking. He was impassive, calm, and he just *radiated* spirituality. Even though he said nothing, after five minutes or so she realised that all her problems were just like a feather that lights on one's arm and can be blown away with the lightest of breaths. At the end of the meeting, he fixed her with those deep eyes of his, so deep that you felt you could fall down them like Alice down the well, and gave her a book. She thought it might be a collection of readings, or mantras, or the biography of a holy man, but it turned out to be a Jackie Collins. Jessica hadn't understood, but Rick said straight away that she *must* read it because Teacher knew so much more about their minds than either of them did. And do you know what? She read it, and she *saw*. She saw how men and women become stuck in the material world as if glued to it, and how, if only they could raise their eyes, they would see the ladder of spiritual ascent, and see that God was everywhere, looking after everyone.

The next paragraph was full of *holy resonances* and *karma*; I skipped to the end, for only then did she mention Amanda and Charles.

They were, she wrote, two healthy, strong teen-agers, with the right diet, the right thoughts, the right surroundings. It was so, *so* different from her own adolescence; she felt it was better to grow up in such a caring community than it was to grow among a cramped, purblind people on the fringe of England, where it was usually cold, it often rained, and there seemed no hope and little future. She was thinking of changing their names, if they agreed – Charles already got Chuck from most of the Americans, anyway. Well, to be honest, she thought Indian names would be more suited to them now. She thought maybe they should *all* have Indian names. They'd found their place in the cosmos, their point on the great wheel. All of them prayed that someday I'd find mine, before it was too late. I was to forget my prejudices – I needed a teacher as well.

I folded the letter and slid it into the rack on the sideboard. There were three others there already, each sent at intervals of about a week.

I went outside to the shelter where I stored wood. When I looked across the dunes I could see the mar-ram move in great swathes as the wind depressed then lifted it. Some weeks ago a large spar had been washed up onto the beach and I had roped and dragged it across the reserve like some biblical slave. I was still sawing it. It lay on trestles in the lee of the shelter, which was merely three wooden walls, buttressed against the storms, and a corrugated-iron roof. I kept all my logs there, although they were often wet and I brought them into the cottage to dry for a few days before I burned them. I took the saw from its hook, touched the teeth with the ball of my thumb and began to work.

At half-past eleven the coastal train, a four-carriage diesel, went down the line. There were only about a dozen passengers on it, staring out of the windows as if hypnotised by the long stretches of shining sand and the grey, broken sea. Two children waved at me, hesitantly, and I waved back at them. When I was a boy children always waved from trains, but they seemed surprised, as if I had been the only one to return their greetings.

I finished the spar and for the next ten minutes I walked round the cottage to see what needed done. I would have to repaint the windows soon, and a slate had slipped on the roof, just above my bedroom. I would have to get the ladder to fix it.

When Celia arrived I was ready for her. Even though she saw me from some distance away, just as soon as she had driven beneath the viaduct, she could not resist pipping her horn.

I had always thought of Celia as a handsome woman, although I had never been attracted to her in anything other than an impersonal sense. She had short, grey hair, clear eyes and a strong jaw. She liked large ornate earrings, and bought her clothes from upmarket chain stores in Newcastle, Manchester and, occasionally, London. The worst remark I had heard about her was that she was mutton dressed as lamb, but I admired her even though she made me feel unnecessarily staid. With her I could not resist playing the hermit. It was an easy option.

I put my article on the dashboard in its envelope. 'I'm sure not many people will read it,' I said.

'Who knows?' she asked. 'It's amazing what people will read. That's the beauty of the regions. Some people will read their local paper from cover to cover – adverts for cars, fatstock prices, WI meetings. You wouldn't get that with the *Sunday Times* now, would you?'

My article was about the flint sites on the reserve, and was to a large extent a paraphrase of a scholarly paper, sent to me by its author, an eager young man who had spent time on the dunes two years ago. He had sifted through the tiny slivers of stone and told me their significance. I had given him full acknowledgement and asked for my meagre payment to be given to charity. I couldn't imagine that many people would persevere beyond the second paragraph. Even though Celia had said I was free to colour the material as much as I wanted, and to speculate on the characteristics of neolithic society, I had not done so. Often, when I take parties of children on guided tours of the reserve, I try to make things more immediate for them. At the flint bed I talk about fear and superstition, how religious thinking was grounded in the unknown and the terrifying. I was certainly not going to put that kind of thing into print; I had had enough of letters to the editor.

Celia and I exchanged small talk and pleasantries, with minutes of silence between, until we got to the pub. This had been built at a crossroads.

The car park was unsurfaced, and there were distinctively-shaped pools of water where rain had gathered in the marks of tractor tyres. We had to bend our heads as we went through the front door, and wipe our feet on a ragged square of coconut matting. Inside there was neither lounge nor bar, but a long room with a coal fire at one end. Two farm labourers, one with a Jack Russell at his heels, talked beside the fire. We sat at the far end.

Celia insisted on placing our order; I sat with half a bitter and waited for the sandwiches. She had a martini and lemonade which she made a wry mouth at as soon as she had taken her first sip.

'Well?' I asked.

She smiled, reached into her handbag and brought out an envelope, holding it so that I could see the stamp. 'From Australia,' she said.

'This is from Toft?' I asked.

'Croft,' she corrected me. The envelope had been opened with a slit as keen as a surgical cut. Celia tilted it, and four black-and-white photographs slipped from it into her hand. She passed them over without comment.

They were photographs of a shifting crowd of people, men and women with oriental faces – each photograph taken with seconds of the others although it was difficult to tell what sequence they were in. In most the figures were crammed together, jostling shoulder to shoulder within the frame. Each face seemed to be suffering some kind of pain or anguish, their eyes narrowed or staring. It looked as though an invisible pressure was beating them down. Some looked as though they were shouting, others as if they were pleading or in despair. On some of the photographs heads had been turned away, as if from a blow. Only one face was common to all the photographs. A face like that of a drowning person just broken surface, the face of a young woman with black hair who strained and fought within the throng. On one photograph her hands were raised but empty, on another they were obscured by someone else's lifted hands. In two photographs she hugged something close to her chest. Her black hair was lifted like a breaking wave, as if a gale had taken it.

'This is why you think I should have something to do with it?' I asked.

Celia was watching my every move. 'That's right, Maurice.'

I shrugged. 'I've no idea what this is. I've seen hundreds, thousands of photographs from Vietnam. Like everyone else, I've seen too much.'

'But you were so good with our local family. Everyone said what a fine job you did settling them into the community.'

'These are Boat People?'

'Could be, he doesn't say. He wants to trace the woman.'

'This one?' I looked at her again. There was nothing to distinguish her from the thousands who had fled. She was in her early twenties, I judged; possibly younger, and probably quite attractive. It was difficult to tell. 'She's not one of our local family. That's not Mrs Thuc, and she's the wrong age for the grandmother. I'm presuming it was taken, what, ten, fifteen years ago? Is that all he says?'

'Bear with me on the photographs, Maurice. Just for a minute. There's something familiar about them, isn't there? Something that tells you you should recognise them?'

I shrugged.

'They're professional. That's obvious. And yet they don't appear to have a centre, do they?'

'So?'

She smiled. I hated playing games.

12

'Just tell me,' I said wearily.

There was a hint of self-satisfaction in her voice. 'No professional would let those out like that. They've been cropped, and badly. The thing that would have given them balance, point, style has been scissored off.' She had put the envelope on the table in front of her, and now she tapped it with one red finger-nail. 'Our Mr Croft is giving us only a few pieces of the jigsaw.'

'Let me read the letter, Celia.'

The paper was coarse, with an elaborately embossed letterhead. I guessed that the Sydney hotel named on it was not as grand as it tried to present itself. Out of habit, I almost raised the paper to my nostrils, but stopped myself just in time. It was written in a regular, neat hand, although there was a pronounced slope to the lettering; the crosspieces of the *t*'s were angled sharply upwards, and the tails of the *y*'s cut down further than was needed.

It was short and to the point. Luciano Croft was the adoptive father of a Vietnamese girl, Kim, now sixteen. He had reason to believe the woman in the photographs could help him trace the girl's natural parents, from whom she had been separated as a child. He and Kim intended to be in England this summer, basing themselves in London but able and willing to travel if necessary. He understood there was a family living in the North-West, the Thucs,

13

but he had not been able to find out their address. They were one of a number of families he was trying to trace, each of whom might be able to give him important information. He had often found that the local press was able and willing to be involved. If they could tell him anything, perhaps they could reply to the address at the bottom of the page.

'The American Embassy,' I said.

'Quite a story?' she suggested.

'There must be thousands like it. The whole world is littered with refugees of one kind or another, many of them trying to find out where their mothers, brothers, nieces are. Peoples have been scattered like the tribes of Israel.'

The sandwiches arrived and Celia paid for them. We began to eat.

'That's so,' she said after a while, 'but this case is rather distinctive. Croft seems to be roaming the world trying to find the natural parents of his daughter. Doesn't that impress you? Doesn't it tug at your heart?'

'Heart? I've been accused of not having one.'

'Please, Maurice, we've talked a lot about you. This time let's talk about Croft.'

She was right. Despite my caution I had often talked, even if obliquely, about nothing but myself when I was alone with her.

'You see this as a story?' I asked, 'syndication, and all that?'

'I haven't seen it in the press, and yet it has all the ingredients – pathos, loss, determination. Even politics.'

'That's not an answer.'

She had her mouth full; a thin trail of liquid escaped from one corner as she smiled, and shone in the light like the path of a snail. She wiped it from her skin with a paper napkin. 'How nice of you to think me so mercenary,' she said. 'I've handed the letter to you, Maurice, because I thought you might be the man to follow it up.'

'I've told you that I stopped being a Good Samaritan years ago. Don't you remember? You covered the story.'

She was jovial with mock exasperation. 'Come off it, I didn't call you Reverend just for a joke. You're the kind of person who should go out of his way to help someone like this. Don't you think he deserves some help?'

'Possibly.'

'Look, you can't complain about the *News*. We were very fair to you when you retired. I have no intention, just yet, of using this letter, although of course I recognise its potential. All I'm asking is a personal question, one friend to another – are you going to help this man and his child?'

'I don't know whether I can. You want me to approach the Thucs, I suppose.'

'They may know the woman. They may hold the key that would unlock – ' she checked the name in the letter ' – Kim's past.'

I looked again at the photographs. There was nothing other than nationality to link them with the Thucs. 'A wild-goose chase, more like,' I suggested, and spread the prints out on the table.

Celia looked at them. 'The mother?' she asked.

'He doesn't say so.'

'Deliberately?'

'That's mere speculation. All right, I'll go and see the Thucs, if that's what you want.' Even as I spoke I had a sense of regret, and felt that I should have held out. The Thucs were no longer anything to do with me.

Her face showed a trace of satisfaction. 'I knew you would. You're a good man, Maurice. Even the Thucs will know that. After what they went through they have every right to be wary. I doubt if they'd trust me.'

'Maybe not. But I warn you, this will be a dead end. I'm certain of it.'

'Worth a try, though? Poor Luciano, he needs a break.' I must have looked unhappy, because she laughed and placed her hand upon my wrist. 'I understand you better than most, Maurice. You're a man who needs constant reassurance. No wonder you left the church. I bet you got depressed just because God didn't answer you every day.'

She could not resist laughing loudly at her own flippancy. But I thought the exaggeration harsh. It was the silence of God, the vast emptiness of the beyond, that had finally led me to break with the life I had led for forty years. Many years before, I had begun to question then reject those very things that were the supports of many people's faith. Some had been easy to lose, for they were recognisable as accretions, myth, dogma. But when I told my congregation that they should accept a Christ who was secular, human, and dead beyond recall, they called me a traitor and a fool.

Since those days I had lived as warden on my reserve, in a cottage belonging to a charitable trust. I logged the comings and goings of birds, mammals, plants; I guided school parties and lectured them on ecology, pollution and natural history; I wrote letters to wildlife magazines and occasionally a piece on the reserve for Celia's paper. I was away from all controversy on my little patch of land.

It was a kind of exile.

That afternoon I followed the remains of the fox tracks across the reserve. A strong wind hummed across the dunes, bending the grasses landwards, smelling of brine, carrying with it the piping of oystercatchers and the break and surge of the waves.

I followed the trail northward, walking parallel to the strand. Where the wind had scoured the sand the pawmarks had vanished, but I came across their traces on the lee side of rises and in sheltered places such as the path through the thicket of sea buckthorn. Planted so that it would stabilise a fragile section of the reserve, the buckthorn had encroached rapidly on the path so that the spikes often brushed my arms if I walked carelessly. I would have to cut it back.

Just beyond the thicket there was a sandy bowl whose surface had been disturbed. As I stepped into it, the soft rim gave beneath my heel. Rabbit prints crisscrossed the bowl, and at the far side its flank had been dug away by the fox. The sand had been flung all around the dig as it worked, and a ragged scoop torn from the incline as if a shelter had been ransacked. Nothing else could be seen, although I knew the rabbit would not be far away. I found it among the marram just above its hide. All its flesh had gone and the fur was turned inside out as if by a butcher.

I topped the broad grassy ridge that rose between the depressions, and looked up the shoreline with my binoculars. The gulls showed no sign of disturbance, and there was no earthy, hot smell lingering on the banks. But, at some distance, a crow flapped upwards from white objects scattered on the beach.

A little further and I could see where the fox had stopped to scratch itself. There were sinuous marks where its haunches had sunk into the sand, although by now the impression had been softened and blurred. Fifty yards on was a disturbance where the snout had been used to push sand into position. I knelt and slid my hand beneath the surface. Almost at once it touched feathers.

I grasped the dead gull and pulled it free. It was stiff, its wings half-open, and sand lodged in the fox's jaw-marks. This one had been a straggler, several hundred yards from the edge of the gullery. I threw it aside for the crows and the ants, for I had an obscure hope that the fox would not return if its larder had been raided.

A further kill made, the fox had headed for the main concentration of prey. The gulls rose at my approach, reeling in the air with furious wings, beaks open as they screamed. I held up a hand to ward them off. Near to their nests, among emptied fragments of shell, there were three adults with broken backs.

On this tip of the reserve, where the sea met the river, the surface was partly of soil, and coarse turf had rooted there. The fox prints vanished among the nests, but I only had to walk the lip of the promontory to see that it had gone along its edge, killing birds until it became tired. Black-headed gulls, aggressive by day, are so docile at night that they can be lifted from their nests by hand. There were fifteen corpses along the strand, strewn among the mussel shells, resting on the black seaweed. After this the fox must have returned through the grasses and followed the river back to its earth on the far side of the railway.

I continued along the beach, back towards the hide.

Ten years ago, when the hut was first placed on the reserve, it had been near the edge of the gullery. My predecessor had sat inside and made notes on the birds' behaviour. Now the gullery had shrunk, and the hide opened onto featureless dunes, a long depression of sand, and the flint bed. The bed itself was unremarkable, being little more than an area of pebbles, stones, and chippings. All the better finds had been taken away to the museums.

I used the hide quite a lot, and often spent several hours there. I had a comfortable wooden seat, a shelf with books, a small gas heater, a plastic container full of water which I used to make tea. Sometimes I had taken refuge there from squalls; often I had opened the shutters, which are hinged at the top, and looked out. After a while rabbits might come running across the sand, or I might see a lizard basking in the sun. When I left, I always made sure I locked the door. Sometimes strangers came onto the reserve at night – courting couples, usually; I did not want to provide them with shelter.

The hide was secure; I checked the lock but did not go in. Afterwards I took my time walking through the grass back towards the cottage.

That night I went into my bedroom and opened my file of photographs. There, among pictures of my younger self, my dead wife, Jessica and the grandchildren, was a photograph of the Thucs. It had been taken on the day the Council had given them the keys to their house. The Mayor's ornate chain of office was silver against his dark suit, almost as if he had turned his body to the lens so the light would make it sharp and clear. The Thucs smiled fixedly and unhappily as they stood in the bizarre assemblages of tropical shirts, cardigans and old coats they had been given. The grandmother stood, partly bent, her fingers curled out of black mitts like shoots escaping to the light, her collapsed face showing no emotion at all. I stood at the end of the line, both proud and guilty, as if I had been compromised by the very presence of these people who had come half way round the world, propelled by chance, to fetch up in my parish.

I could remember the day quite clearly. The Mayor made a little speech, members of the Council and voluntary bodies gave a thin but vigorous burst of applause, the photographer from Celia's paper clicked as the keys were handed over in a ceremony which the Thucs seemed to only part understand. Coached by me, they did their best to show how grateful they were, inclining their heads in truncated bows as if it was the only gesture they had learned. A number of curious locals stood looking on as though witnessing a ritual devoid of meaning.

I took Croft's photographs from their envelope and placed them beside the faces of the Thucs. The only resemblances I saw were racial.

Afterwards I sat by the fire and listened to Radio 3. I was beginning to feel uneasy about my promise to Celia. I had forced myself to stay away from the Thucs. They had seemed both betrayed and exotic, their needs so great and their journey so dangerous. Even though I had not liked them, I found myself taking more and more time to look after them. Not only had I helped them get the house, I had also guided and instructed them on household appliances and fuel bills, social services, rent; I had introduced them to schools and doctors, arranged that a voluntary teacher of English work with them for six months. I had even organised several job interviews for Mr Thuc. I became too much of a father to them. I was over-protective, always on hand, perhaps more for my own peace of mind than for their actual needs. And I believed that, after a while, I had begun to detect in them the resentment that begins to build like silt in a harbour among those who are dependent on such patronage. Even though I had volunteered to go to see them, I had no idea how the Thucs would welcome me.

2

IT WAS ALMOST A WEEK BEFORE I WENT TO SEE THEM. I used to have a life organised and given shape by services, school boards, councils, christenings, marriages, burials. Now that I had my reserve, and little else, my days were shaped by the weather, tides, migrations, the visits of predators. All that week, as I walked the ebbing levels, I could see translucent bristled tubes the size of cartridges being washed up by the sea. The damp sand was littered with them. I knew they were the emptied shells of burrowing worms, but never before had there been such quantities of them. It was as if some great change, possibly a disaster, had happened beneath the waters. I spent my time speculating on this, and letting shallow waves send the tubes tumbling over my boots, rather than force myself to think about Luciano Croft and his letter.

One day, as I walked back toward the cottage, I could hear the phone ringing. I knew it would be Celia, so I waited and did not go in until it had stopped. Afterwards I hung up my coat and took off my boots. It was time to go and see the Thucs. I did not want Celia to ring again.

It took me half an hour to drive to town, following the coast road. The Thucs had been placed in a housing estate on the hump of land that rose above the harbour. There were five hundred houses or more, each with a grey slate roof, walls of grey pebbledash, and an open-plan front garden where the only flowers were in thin strips under the windows. On the very crest of the hill was a factory with tall chimneys, white vapour streaming away from them in the westerly breeze.

I locked the car and, slightly nervous, went up the path to the front door. It was answered by the son. The last time I had seen him was a few years ago, when he had been part of a guided tour I had taken round the dunes. Now he had grown taller and stronger. His black hair was cut in a style favoured by adolescents of his age group, and he wore a jacket covered in metal badges. As it swung I could hear them clink like milkbottle tops blown down a road. He looked momentarily perplexed and, because I did not quite recognise him for a moment, I was not the first to speak.

'Yes?'

'Ky,' I said, extending my hand. As I did so I wondered if he would consider a handshake inappropriate; I had not seen many young people shake hands.

He shook it quickly, as if embarrassed.

'Maurice Fretwell,' I said, in case he could not remember my name. 'Are you still at school?'

He cleared his throat nervously. 'Exams this summer,' he said. His accent was surprisingly local, although worn a little more lightly than if he had been born here. I nodded approvingly. He looked at me incuriously, and did not offer to let me pass.

'It's your parents, or perhaps your grandmother, who might be able to help me. Are they in?'

He stepped back and I walked through the hall and into the sitting-room. A huge television set was turned on in one corner, but there was no sound coming from it. A three-piece suite and too many chairs were packed onto the carpet, which ended just short of the skirting boards. An upright piano, secondhand, had been placed against one wall, and above it were two brightly-coloured prints showing vaguely oriental scenes of stylised mountains and romanticised peasants.

Ky's mother came out of the kitchen, followed by his grandmother. Mrs Thuc wore a blue mohair cardigan, blue strands sticking out from it as if it had been electrified, but the grandmother wore black, almost as if she were still living in her own country, although I noticed that on her feet were a pair of fur-lined zip-up boots. Mrs Thuc looked at me as if she did not quite know what to do. Behind her the grandmother bent forward and then back, but even when fully erect she was still as curved as a figure on a medieval clock. 'How are you both?' I asked, enunciating clearly and loudly. I had always addressed the Thucs as if from a lectern and I was still not sure how much they would understand.

'Hello,' Mrs Thuc said, the word rustling in her throat. She motioned me to sit down. I sat on the nearest chair with my feet underneath the seat for there was hardly any room to stretch them out. Out of the corner of my eye I saw Ky attempt to leave, but his mother must have called him back, for, after a sudden burst of speech from her, he sat down, morosely, at the other side of the room.

'Are you all well? I haven't seen you for a long time. I hope you've all settled in now. And Mr Thuc?'

Mrs Thuc nodded. I could see her thinking of a response, but the words must have been difficult.

'He's at work,' Ky said. I had to ask before he told me that Mr Thuc had a job at the factory. Not a good one, but one which brought in a reasonable wage. Mrs Thuc had wanted a job too, but no one would employ her. I nodded understandingly. All the time Mrs Thuc stared fixedly at me, her face set in a waxwork smile. I found it difficult to meet her gaze. I wondered if she thought they were living in a kind of purgatory, and that I had helped force them into it.

'And you, Ky?' I asked.

He shrugged.

'What do you want to do?'

'I want to make money,' he replied, with startling frankness.

'You enjoyed your trip to the reserve, I remember. Are you still interested in wildlife?'

He shook his head angrily, as if I had reminded him of a past failure. I looked at his jacket, thinking that perhaps there would be a name I would recognise among the badges. There were none. Just tiers of surreal and barbaric names.

I forced myself to look at Mrs Thuc, and then at the grandmother, who looked at me askance from her inclined face. 'Mrs Thuc, I've come to see if you can help. You and your family. I've come to ask a favour.' Their expressions did not change, and I appealed to Ky. 'Perhaps you could translate?'

He shrugged, then spoke in the high, undifferentiated tones of his native tongue. His mother nodded slowly and, I thought, warily.

'Look,' I said, taking Croft's letter from my pocket, 'this arrived a few days ago at the newspaper offices. It's from someone asking for help.' I waited while Ky translated. 'He's been all over the world looking for the real parents of a girl who was born in your country about sixteen years ago. He doesn't know anything about her. I don't think he even knows her true name. But he thinks that the Vietnamese community in Britain may be able to help.' While Ky spoke I took out the letter and held it open, so that they could take it and look at it if they wished. No one did.

Mrs Thuc had sat down in a peculiarly stiff posture. The grandmother had turned and was beginning to walk back into the kitchen.

'He thinks this woman may know something.' I slid the photographs out of the envelope and passed them to Mrs Thuc. I did not want to appear to be putting her under any kind of pressure, so I glanced aside as she looked at them. As soon as she took them, however, she began to speak rapidly, and I turned to see her pass them over to Ky. There was a new expression on her face, but I could not tell what it was. Relief, possibly, or annoyance.

Ky took them and glanced idly at them. 'My mother says she would help the man if she could, but this face means nothing to her.' The mother spoke again. 'None of them do,' Ky added.

'She's certain?'

'Of course she is,' he said with sudden assurance, 'otherwise she would have said.'

I was momentarily abashed, but knew I had to continue. Celia would ask me everything that had gone on. 'And your grandmother?'

'She does not know,' Mrs Thuc suddenly said, her voice brittle.

'But she hasn't seen the prints, Mrs Thuc.'

Mrs Thuc shook her head vigorously and spoke to Ky. He held the photographs out to me, but I did not take them. 'She says they've never seen her before in their lives. They don't know who she was.'

'Was? Why do they think she's dead?'

For a moment I felt, unjustly, like a detective trapping a suspect. But, after a short exchange, Ky replied calmly, 'She guessed the woman must be dead by now because so many are. Isn't she?'

'I don't know.' The photographs were still being proffered, but still I ignored them. 'He's an American' I said. 'Someone in Australia must have given him your name and said you might be able to help.'

They still refused to have anything to do with Croft's plea.

'Look,' I said a little desperately, 'Mr Thuc will be back soon, won't he?'

'First shift,' his wife said, as if I had triggered a reflex.

'I'll leave the prints here. Is that all right? Maybe he will know the woman. Perhaps, after a while, you'll think that maybe you can give us some information. I don't know who she was – an old neighbour, someone from the boats or a transit camp, a distant relative that only Mr Thuc would recognise. I'll call back for them in a couple of days. Is that all right?'

They did not seem to want to accept even this, but after I had restated my case, and pleaded especially hard with them, they agreed with reluctance. Ky handed the photographs back to his mother who immediately dropped them face-down on top of the piano.

Ky showed me out. I felt tired and annoyed at myself for having become involved. At the door I paused. 'Do you have trouble from people round here, Ky?'

He shuffled and looked down. 'Sometimes.'

'What – names shouted, stones thrown?'

'That sort of thing. But some of them are mates of mine. I understand why it happens. And some say we should be the last to complain.'

'I wouldn't say that, Ky.' I shook his hand again. He appeared rather embarrassed, but obviously had something on his mind, and I noticed him hesitate before he spoke. 'Yes?' I asked, to encourage him.

'About what you call me.'

I did not know what he meant.

'Everyone calls me Keith now.'

I nodded. 'Of course,' I said.

By the time I had taken a few steps down the path he was already closing the door.

After visiting the Thucs I drove into town and parked near the law courts. There was only one space available and the clearance was narrow, but I was lucky to have found it so I inched the car between two others. I was so close to the next car that I could not open my own door fully and had to get out awkwardly.

As I was doing this I saw Ratcliffe walking towards me, although he had not seen me as yet. I guessed that he was on his way to give evidence, for he was wearing a good suit and a new shirt. His measured pace would take him right past my parking place, and for a moment I wondered if I should stoop low inside my car and pretend to look for something so that he would pass by without seeing me. Before I could make a move, however, our eyes met.

'Reverend,' he said, with a kind of clinical cheeriness, 'I haven't seen you for a long time. How are you?'

'Inspector,' I said.

We shook hands too quickly, as if each of us was glad to be rid of the formality. There was no warmth in his handshake, merely a kind of muscular social efficiency. It had been some time since I had been close to Ratcliffe, and his face had coarsened. His clothes were more expensive, though, and better cut. I had the impression that he wished to appear fastidious and unapproachable except on his own terms, like a successful surgeon, but he had neither the wealth nor the sleekness. Perhaps aware of such a shortfall, he had become both more friendly and more sly. Nicotine stained his fingers and the third finger of his right hand was adorned with an ornate gypsyish ring which appeared far too flamboyant for a policeman. He had the air of a boxer who had prospered not by skill but by cunning.

'Celia Price tells me you spend most of your time watching seagulls now,' he said.

'That sort of thing. You see Celia a lot, I suppose.'

'She's often taking notes. The reporters have a rota; she takes her turn.'

'Will she be there today? I was going to see her at the *News*.'

'Ah, another of your articles, is it? I've seen them, but never read them. Well, they're not my kind of thing, really. You're not offended, are you?'

'Not at all. I see your name all the time in the court reports.'

'A policeman's lot, Maurice. If I see her, I'll tell her I've met you.'

'It's not important; I can ring her. Who knows about court cases, anyway – they could be any kind of length. What is it today?'

'A rape. Rather sordid, I'm afraid – threatened the girl with a knife, punched her a lot. One of our local boys, too.'

'Would I know anyone?'

'I don't think so,' he said, and gave an unexpected and disquieting smile. 'They're both Catholics, not C of E.'

'They knew each other?'

'According to his priest, he was a good lad until this. He was even friendly with the girl, in a distant kind of way. Still, you never can tell with people.'

'No.'

Ratcliffe looked at his watch. 'Must go,' he said. But instead of moving he looked closely at me.

'What's wrong?' I asked.

He shook his head. 'Nothing,' he said, and we parted.

A few minutes later I stopped in front of a shop with a mirror and looked at my reflection, but I could see nothing wrong with myself. I was no less healthy than usual.

To people such as me Ratcliffe was always keen to give the impression of consideration and helpfulness. I had come to see him, however, as a person whose job, and that alone, gave him focus. Like all policemen he worked to a set of defined rules and procedures, and all that he did, all that he thought, was subordinate to this. During the Edmondson tragedy our relationship had become almost painfully ironic. For me, the accident had precipitated a crisis, and I had had to face at last the truth about my relationship with the church, its tenets, its ritual. Ratcliffe had been sympathetic to the Edmondsons and to me, but his official testimony spoke only of the loss of the girl, the search, the discovery of the body. It was as if the entire event could be reduced to a formula, a code. For him, the Edmondsons had neglected the most simple of rules, and let the girl wander away to her death. For me, the fact of her death had a profound moral aftermath.

After an hour or so shopping, I loaded the car boot and went to a small Italian restaurant I had sometimes visited when I was a vicar. It had changed hands and the new owners did not recognise me. It was relaxing to be able to sit in a corner and eat a quiet lunch. I had just handed my payment to the waiter when Celia came in, looking round until she saw me.

'I thought you might be here,' she said, pulling back a chair and sitting down. The waiter came with my change on a saucer and looked inquiringly at her, but she waved him away and he retreated, pulling a face. 'Harry Ratcliffe said he'd seen you, and I guessed you might be here at this time of day. Do you remember, just before you resigned, we sat and talked here? At this very table?'

She was right. I had forgotten, or more likely suppressed the memory, but now it came back to me with extraordinary force – the sunlight coming through the horizontal blinds onto the breadfruit leaves, the wicker chair becoming uncomfortable, empty wineglasses on the table, Celia and I, a hand's breadth between us, talking about what I should do. I had felt so misjudged, so depressed, that it was as if the temperature in the room had dipped and a shadow crossed the sun. The whole town had been full of exaggerated rumour about what I had said to the Edmondsons.

'And how was Inspector Ratcliffe?' I asked sardonically.

'Playing everything by the book, as usual. I've never seen him caught out, not even by the wiliest defence. He constructs a good case, I'll give him that.'

'What that has to do with the truth I'm not sure,' I said. 'I never have been. I always thought that he would do anything to achieve his own ends.'

'Especially when they're lawful ones,' Celia said drily and, with a change of tone that signified a move to another subject, '*You*, Maurice, are going to tell me about the Thucs.' There was the trace of a smile, a tiny smirk, that made me suspicious.

'I've seen them. They know nothing about the woman and none of them has ever seen her. I can't be sure about Mr Thuc, but I've left the prints there so he can look at them.' I looked at Celia and she nodded. 'All right?'

'*They* may never have seen her,' she said, failing to keep the triumph from her voice, 'but I have.'

I was genuinely surprised and must have shown it, for her grin broadened.

'You know Maurice,' she went on, 'I love shocking you. You're so prim, so solemn. If you were holy, you'd be holier-than-thou. Come on, let's go.'

It was only ten minutes walk to the newspaper office, which was up a sidestreet near the market-place. On the way Celia explained to me that one of her old contacts had come up with something interesting. Every so often she reminded me of her time in Manchester. I had thought that, as with so many of us, her life had not gone quite the way she had planned it. Twenty years ago, sitting in a Northern sub-office and having the occasional piece taken by Fleet Street, she must have thought that her tenacity, her way with words, her ability to cajole and wheedle would take her to London and beyond. Once, she had confessed that she was so certain this would happen that she let everything become subservient to her intended career. Now, like me, she had become beached in this remote corner of England, disliking it and yet constantly fascinated by it. Only in her sharper moments must she have wondered what had gone wrong, and which of the many turnings she had taken had been the fatal one. To disguise her own feelings she now pretended that Manchester had been an aberration, a skirmish with those forces of size, mercenariness and impersonality which she most disliked about her profession. Secretly, she must have wondered in her heart of hearts if she could ever be taken back into such company.

When I had been a vicar, and a regular visitor to the *News* office, there had been a long, mahogany counter which reminded me of the counter at a nearby grocer's when I was a boy. There had been large books the size of atlases, an old clock with a white face that had lost its shine, and an Edwardian card-calendar that was adjusted each day. Now the front part of the office was open-plan, with an enquiries desk, a mustard-yellow carpet, and girls working on word processors, the brightness turned up so high that a greenish tinge showed on their skins.

Celia took me into her office. There was an untidy stack of papers on her desk. The shelves were full of reference books, many of which, she told me, she had bought herself. A vase with Japanese dried flowers was stuck in the window, and a photograph of her parents lay collapsed but face up in its frame on top of some green Roneo cabinets.

I sat down in the chair opposite hers while she unlocked her desk and passed a plastic file over to me. 'Exhibit one,' she said, obviously self-satisfied.

I opened the file. Inside were three photocopied pieces from Australian newspapers. Each of them had a photograph, which the copying had coarsened and turned into high contrast so that the faces of the subjects had become as simplified as carnival masks. Even so, I could tell that the man was lean, with cropped hair and possibly balding, and that his face was strong but inexpressive. Beside him the girl was slight, fragile, her hair the colour of deepest carbon, her mouth and nose tiny, and eyes that were like the black circles of cartoons.

'From Australia House?'

'One of my old contacts works there now. It was easy, really.'

Two of the reports were similar, and written in like prose. Luciano Croft, son of an Italian mother and a Montana farmer, was the adoptive father of a Vietnamese girl whom he had called Kim. After his wife's death in an accident he had begun to follow a trail across the world that he hoped would lead to Kim's parents. *I did my time in Vietnam*, he was reported as saying, *many of the people I knew are either dead or have been scattered across the surface of the globe. I'm doing what I can to bring two halves of a family together.* They had been following leads throughout Australia, particularly among the settlements of Boat People; after that, he didn't know where they would go, but there were a number of possibilities he could follow. He would never stop until he could find out who Kim's parents were and what had happened to them.

The other report concentrated on Kim. Here, despite the roughness of the copy, I could see that the photographer had caught her as both vulnerable and precocious. Across the top of the frame, in bold blocks, were the words *Heartbreak Kim's Mission Of Love.* 'Not your style, Maurice?' Celia asked. 'You should read it anyway.'

Lovely Kim Croft thinks she's sixteen. She can't be sure. The date of her birth has vanished along with her parents, her brothers and her sisters in the maelstrom that was the end of democratic Saigon. Now, ebony-haired, almond-eyed Kim follows her adoptive father across five continents in a

*heartbreaking quest for her origins. She still calls 'Lucky'
Croft Dad, though. 'He's been wonderful to me,' Kim
told me as she sipped a Pepsi overlooking the waterfront,
'I owe him everything. Nothing upsets him and nothing
will stand in his way. He'll find my family if it's the
last thing he does.' Meanwhile, young men walked past
her several times but Kim never gave them a second
glance. She has a bigger goal, one she won't recognise
at first, and she doesn't know if it will be in the back
streets of Sydney or somewhere far out of sight beyond
the next horizon.*

I handed the clipping back to her. 'A little over-wrought for me,' I said.

'A man driven, though?'

'Sounds like it.'

Celia placed the papers between her elbows and
leaned forward, interlacing her fingers. 'Let me ask
you a question. How did those two meet?'

Her expression did not change, but there was a
hint of pleasure in her voice. I knew the question
was not idle.

'I don't know. But you have another report, don't
you?'

'Not exactly. Why do you think Croft and his
wife adopted her? As a charitable act?'

'It was fashionable for a while. After the baby
airlift. Whole planeloads of them were brought out
just before Saigon fell.'

'It could have been because of what he did in the war. He admits he was there. Does Kim assuage his guilt?'

'Speculation again, Celia. It has no real value.'

'You're a religious man, Maurice. You know all about redemption, expiation, guilt.'

I leaned back in the chair so I was further away from her. '*Used* to be,' I corrected her. Then I added 'Perhaps Mr Croft is doing this from a sense of duty.'

'Would you say goodness, as well?'

I nodded without overemphasis. I was wary of what she might say.

'Isn't it interesting how we want to believe that goodness and morality are still at work in the world, Maurice? That those great abstractions are still detectable as a silver thread running through our tangled, messy little lives?'

I did not respond, and, as if pleading a cause, she changed her tone again.

'You know, often, if I see a photograph of something familiar I don't recognise it. I saw a landscape shot recently that was cropped so that I didn't recognise it at all – and yet it was of a skyline that I must have looked at hundreds of times. If someone gave you a close-up of part of your reserve you might not know where it was taken.'

'Is this going to be the next exhibit?'

'The girl's mother – '

'We don't know it's her in the photographs. Do we?'

'I knew I'd seen it before, but I couldn't place it. Then, after I got those cuttings, I began to remember. And I was wrong. I didn't know Croft's photographs. I knew the one he *didn't* send.' She took a large book from the rack. 'This had been gathering dust, I'm afraid, although it's considered essential reading – one of our bibles, if you'll forgive that word. Lots of examples – how to select, display, crop.' She held the spine toward me so that I could read it; *Principles Of Photojournalism*.

'She's in there?'

'The very same.'

She had the page marked with a piece of paper. She opened the book, turned it in her hands and laid it on the desk top in front of me. On the left-hand side were four small photographs, each taken within a few seconds of the other. Areas of strength and weakness were highlighted by stylised circles and obliques across the prints. Within them, occupying about a quarter of each total shot, were Croft's images.

But largest of all was a fifth photograph, the one I knew Celia would have recognised, the one Croft must have chosen not to send us. As soon as I saw it I recalled it myself, and my chest felt unaccountably hollow. A helicopter lifted off, its dark interior crammed with passengers; the blades a mere blur of shadow and sky. A shocked young American leaned out of the bay at a dangerous angle, his hands half-outstretched, seemingly frozen in mid-air. Just out of reach, her face distorted by anguish, a woman held out a bundle to him. To one side of the bundle a tiny hand could be seen.

'It's the girl,' I said. I did not even have to look at the captions to know the place and the date.

'It was when the Americans lifted who they could from the embassy grounds,' Celia said. 'Recognise anything else?'

I had become dull-witted with surprise and gazed without thought at the crowd of heads around the woman with the child.

'The man leaning out of the helicopter,' Celia said, and I stared at the figure. 'It's him, isn't it? Tell me you agree.'

The face was similar to the photocopied face from the Australian newspapers. 'I don't know. It could be.'

'Of course it is. The coincidences are just too great.'

'How can you say that? You're a reporter. Shouldn't you be worried about facts?'

'Lawyers do that. Reporters look for connections. It's the pattern that matters.'

'But the figures are too far apart. She could never have passed the child over in time.'

'I've read up on it. Everything became more and more chaotic. People were coming over the walls, everyone was struggling for a place – the orderly evacuation creaked and fell apart. It must have been a nightmare. Imagine the scramble, the panic – isn't it conceivable that the helicopter settled back down, or dipped? Couldn't someone have said that there was room for one more passenger, one weighing just a few pounds? Look at them; they're not so far apart. And cameras can distort distance anyway.'

I pushed the book back to her. 'You really want it to be them, don't you?'

She nodded.

'Why didn't he send us the main shot, rather than these? If it had really been him, and that was the girl, why didn't he do that?'

'I'll tell you what I think. I can't give you all the answers, but we can assume a certain amount. We can be fairly sure that Luciano Croft was one of the last Americans out of Saigon in April '75. The photograph has a date, so there's no doubt he was there at that time. The limited evacuation, which was really rather large, was the kind of thing you'd expect. The important, the favoured, the rich, the politically sensitive, the undercover men, were all jockeying for positions in the queue. Those left behind were the poor, the naive, the innocent, and the sympathisers. Croft's there at the bay. He doesn't seem to be wearing a uniform, although it's difficult to tell; certainly there were marines guarding the evacuation for almost all

of the time. The helicopters that the Americans called
Jolly Green Giants came in and took people off to the
fleet lying offshore. Each one was crammed to capacity
and beyond. Can't you just picture the scene, Maurice?
The rotor blades chopping the air, the pilot scared he'll
never get the beast off the ground, those on board
packed so tight they can hardly breathe and with
all their belongings jettisoned? Outside a throng of
people clamours and fights for the last few places.
Then, suddenly, a woman holds up her child like an
offering, praying it will be saved. A total stranger, a
young American, stretches out and takes it, possibly
without even knowing why. Some impulse he can't
understand, some humane gesture makes him reach
out and save a life that, at least superficially, has
nothing to do with his own. Years later, the girl
grown, he crisscrosses the world in a journey that
has every reason to be called epic.'

I let the silence hang in the air for a few moments.
I could hear the noise of cars, voices, footsteps outside
in the street. A fly lifted from the windowpane, spun
round the room, then landed back on the glass and
began to crawl up it.

'You sound as if you're writing copy, Celia,' I
said.

'Perhaps.'

'You'd do what you could to write a story like
that, is that what you're trying to tell me?'

44

THE FLINT BED

'I have a suspicion about our friend Croft. I have no evidence for it, just a nose for people. If he thinks we're valuable, he'll use us. If not, he'll turn elsewhere. It's as simple as that.'

'The press, you mean?'

'Yes. Or anyone. These are orchestrated reports; I recognise them. He would do that because he was at a dead-end in Australia, and possibly someone would read the reports and contact him with a lead. But with the Thucs, he *has* a lead. He doesn't need us. Yet. Maybe that explains the photographs that he sent us. They're teasers, that's all. He doesn't want to show his full hand yet.'

'He won't need to. The Thucs want nothing to do with him.'

'You think he would accept that, even if it were true? He'll want to check it himself. He would accept neither your word nor mine if the lead was strong enough. Sooner or later, he'll be here.'

'It'll be a waste of time,' I protested.

'You would love to meet him, though. Wouldn't you? All your working life you must have been searching for someone who was the embodiment of abstract ideals – spiritual love, selfless duty, nobility. Now we have a man who has duty thrust upon him. Quite literally.'

I nodded but without emphasis. Celia had always loved to pursue me on points of arcane theological

45

and moral interest, such as whether Adam had a navel and, if God existed, what was the moral worth to be found in the life cycle of the ichneumon fly. I always protested that these were unimportant and peripheral, but it never blunted her adolescent glee in hounding me. 'I don't think I'm available for comment,' I said.

'The more I think of it, the more I believe it wasn't a reflex. He would even have had time to turn away. What do you think?'

'Is this part of your pattern?'

'Just the worldly one. I leave it to you to consider the metaphysics of his action, and how it forms part of the hidden web that binds everything together.'

'You shouldn't confuse my beliefs with my daughter's, Celia. It becomes wearisome.'

She smiled. 'I don't think so. The ecological structure of the reserve is just a worldly expression of your theological concerns, no matter how many times you may deny it. Tell me, as a man of God – '

'Ex,' I interrupted, not bothering to keep the annoyance from my voice.

' – do you think our Mr Croft had a moment of revelation, a flash of enlightenment? Could he foresee the almost mythic task he was undertaking, the pursuit of someone he might not even recognise across a heartless world?'

'Celia, for a professional fact-finder you're an

incurable romantic. Besides, the discussion is academic. Luciano Croft has no need to come here. We
must write back and tell him that the Thucs cannot
help, assuming Mr Thuc is of the same mind as his
wife. I regret ever having become involved in this, if
you must know. It unsettles me.'

'A stranger asks us for help. We can't deny him
that.'

'Please don't try to give me lessons in morality,
Celia; only the eager would respond to that line of
argument. And, while you're at it, don't raise the
idea of responsibility either. We're not responsible
for arranging a meeting between him and the Thucs.
After today, I'm not even sure it would be wise.'

Celia settled back in her chair and smiled. From
the enquiries area of the office I could hear the noise
of someone agitated and shouting. 'So,' she asked,
'we *are* still helping him, aren't we?'

'Look,' I said, 'let's just let it die.' As I spoke I
realised that I was torn between rejecting Croft and
seeking his approval. To be worthy of someone like
him would have been intriguing, and demanding. I
was not even sure I would want it.

Quite suddenly Celia got up and began to walk
swiftly to the door. I did not understand what she
was doing, but as soon as the door was opened I recognised a heavily-accented voice, made more confused by
excitement. I followed Celia as quickly as I could.

Mr Thuc was standing by the reception desk, his body tensed as if he was about to strike someone. The girl behind the desk was looking distressed and scared, but I could also see incomprehension on her face. In her hand she was holding Croft's letter.

Thuc had never been able to pronounce *reverend*, and had always called me *vicar*. 'Vicar Fretwell,' he said now, mangling my surname in his agitation, 'this is no good. No good!'

Celia walked to him and began to address him smoothly, but he brushed her aside.

'You cannot upset my family like this, vicar Fretwell. Everyone very upset, my wife, my mother-in-law, everyone very upset. This man has nothing to do with us.'

'I'm sorry,' I said, 'I didn't wish to – '

'The war has been over a long time. We are English now. We do not want this man. We do not want his girl. We want to forget all this trouble, all this war. We are happy here.'

'Of course,' Celia said soothingly, 'no one wanted you to be upset. Won't you come inside and sit down? We can talk things over, Mr Thuc. The minister and I were just trying to help Mr Croft.'

Thuc shook his head and took several steps towards the door. 'You were our friend, vicar Fretwell. Why do you make my wife cry like this? We do not know this

Croft. We have never seen him. He is nothing to do with us. Nothing.'

And with that he opened the door and, still shaking his head as if the stupidities of people like me were beyond belief, he stepped out onto the street and let the door crash shut behind him.

3

THE VOICE WAS AMERICAN, QUIET BUT INSISTENT.
Even though it had been three months since his letter,
I immediately thought of Croft. 'Yes?'

'Sir, my name is Luciano Croft. I understand you
may have heard of me.'

'Yes, I have.'

'Do I call you *Mr*? Or is it some church title?'

'Mr will be fine, Mr Croft. Where are you calling from?'

'London.' There was a fractional pause, then he
went on. 'Mr Fretwell, this is damned awkward, but
I'm on a payphone and I don't have many coins. I'll
give you my number. Can you note it down?'

I was slightly annoyed. I did not like my gener-
osity being taken advantage of. And if Croft had
really wanted to talk to me, I felt it would have
been civil of him to make sure it was on my terms,
not on his. Almost as soon as I had finished noting
the figures the line went dead.

I considered not returning the call; considered,
too, leaving the phone off the hook in case, after

a while, he should ring again. If ever he caught up with me I could say I had made a mistake on one of the numbers. But, only a few seconds after we had been disconnected, I dialled. He answered immediately.

'Mr Croft, we have cheap-rate calls after six in this country. Both you and I would have better value then.'

He ignored this. 'You've read my letter. I have a reply here from a lady, name of Celia Price. She tells me you're the man who did all the arrangements for the Thuc family.'

'I've seen her reply. She also says that the Thucs don't think they can help you.'

'I still have to see them, Mr Fretwell.'

'We're a long way from London. Have you seen where we are on a map?'

'I have, and I've talked to your travel people as well. This letter doesn't quote an address for the Thucs, though. Do you have it?'

'I don't think they even want to see you. They certainly showed scant interest in your problem. And it wouldn't be ethical for me to quote their address without their permission. They haven't given that.'

'You've asked them?'

'The question's academic. They don't want to see you. They say.'

'They gave you a reason?'

'I think they just want to forget the war. And they say they're British now.'

'British? So they're on your register of electors?'

I said nothing. Croft was certainly sharp, but I doubted if the Thucs had become naturalised. They would have spent their money on something else.

'You can tell the Thucs I'm on my way, Mr Fretwell. With Kim. I intend to find out just how much they can tell us.'

'You must do as you think fit, Mr Croft.'

'What would you do in my position? Spend the rest of your life, maybe, wondering if you had missed some clue just because you hadn't pushed hard enough? I guess you understand that.'

'Yes,' I said reluctantly, 'I do.'

I could hear him clear his throat. 'Fact is, Mr Fretwell, I need some more of your help.'

'I don't know you, Mr Croft. I don't really know what you look like and I have only a vague idea of what you're doing. You seem to expect help from total strangers.'

Unexpectedly, he began to sound defensive. 'We've travelled half the world. Lots of strangers have helped.'

'Perhaps. Did you tell them the full story? You only told us part of it.'

'How much more do you know?'

'I've seen the photograph. The one you didn't send us.'

There was a silence on the end of the line. I could hear his shallow breathing and, in the background, an undifferentiated murmur which I took to be traffic.

'That told us a lot more than your letter did,' I said.

'Should I do a circular, Mr Fretwell, telling everyone who I am and how I came by Kim? Maybe you think that would do us a lot of good, but my guess is that it wouldn't. People would get diverted, they'd worry about the wrong things, they wouldn't get what I was after at all. Others would come forward because they wanted to be part of the act, they wanted to be involved. I reckon it's best to keep it simple, straight, like a police investigation. I try to use the practical minimum, that's all.'

I saw his point. Perhaps Celia was right. If we failed him, then he would use the press. Suddenly I wondered what would happen if the Thucs had a change of heart and responded to an appeal by Croft in the popular press. Would Celia and I be seen as selfish and unhelpful? In particular, would it confirm people's impression of me as cold, distant, preoccupied with abstraction?

'I still don't see how I can do any more for you,' I said.

'Well,' he replied, drawing out the word as if he was acting in an old Western, 'we have a real need for practical help. Hotels are beyond our pocket at the moment.'

I waited for him to go on.

'In some towns there have been voluntary organisations, welfare, charities. Sympathisers. I'm not a man for receiving charity, Mr Fretwell, but you should know that damn near all my money has gone on this thing.'

'I see.'

'We'd be no trouble.'

'Of course not.' I did not believe him, although I believed his intentions.

'You can maybe think of some way round that difficulty? We'll be up with you next week. I could give you a ring before I set off.'

'After six,' I said.

'Oh, and you needn't tell the Thucs that we'll be arriving. Not if you don't want.'

'I didn't promise you the address, Mr Croft.'

'No,' he said. But I knew that he could find it anyway.

Later a post-office van drew up outside, the sun dazzling on its roof. I walked swiftly to the front door, opening it before the mail could be slipped through the letter-box. The postwoman had almost reached the door, and behind her the car engine was still running. 'Good afternoon, Mrs Edmondson,' I said.

She had a broad, surly face, as red as any farmer's, and her mouth was set with distaste. 'Here,' she said, thrusting the mail at me. She had not called me by my name since her daughter's accident. I took a package and another of Jessica's letters from her. She did not turn on her heel, but stood for a moment, as if waiting for our meeting to somehow resolve itself. I believed that, like me, she sought out meetings even though she had nothing to say. Perhaps she believed that her presence was a constant reminder and reproach; that, seeing her, I would be tortured by guilt, or see the chasms of hell open at my feet. I always did my best to appear untroubled. I wanted her to realise, even if it only came slowly and over years, that what I had said to her was what I believed to be true.

'Thank you,' I said, over-pleasant. 'A letter from my daughter, and a book I ordered on shoreline ecology. It'll be heavy stuff, I'm afraid.'

'Your daughter,' she said flatly.

'That's right.' I refused to be embarrassed, or to disguise the fact.

Mrs Edmondson nodded, and went back to her car. When she drove away she looked straight ahead, not even checking in her mirror. It had been hot for several days, and the car raised dust from the hard but broken mud at the roadside.

Just in front of the house, between my front window and the road, I had placed a wooden bench. On hot days I sat there, turning things over in my mind, sometimes dozing. Once or twice I had fallen asleep and woken with a start out of some vivid dream not knowing where I was. An hour after receiving it, I sat there and read Jessica's latest letter.

The monsoon had been incredibly heavy that year, so heavy that it seemed at times that they would float off on the water as in some children's adventure. But the real adventure was *there*, she said. She told me about walking to see some Indian friends who gave them coconut dipped in sugar, how Rick had his hair cut under a banana tree by a travelling barber, how the rice harvest had been picturesque and sort of pastoral, with women using the entrance hall to their home as a place to shift the grains from the stalks by rolling bundles under their feet. The name changes were still under discussion, apparently; Teacher had said they should think long and hard about such things, for to change a name is to change a person.

Rick's cousin had been killed in a car crash. He had been driving to Seattle for a conference. Rick had said that he would have been very sad if he had been the old Rick, but now Teacher's insight had made him understand these things ever so much better.

At the end of the letter she became direct.

Teacher understands, too, why I write these letters to you with little or no reply. He says I need the expression, the way some writers need it. You may think that

*this is a contradiction, and that I aim for a life with no
such needs. That's true, Dad. I aim to go beyond the self
– beyond pain, beyond need, beyond the world. I'm like a
sailor baling out dirty water to make his craft seaworthy.
Eventually these letters will start to dry up, I guess. Each
of us follows his or her own path. I don't know how long
it will take me to walk mine. I only know the direction
I'm going in.*

When I read passages such as that I felt saddened
and betrayed. I considered Jessica's childhood to
be much better than my own. She had grown up, I
believed, in an atmosphere of comfort and tolerance.
Now she was allowing her own children to grow
in surroundings that were disturbingly alien, and
with teaching that I thought perverse, mystifying
and feudal.

My boyhood was spent among dank rows of
back-to-backs with slate roofs, lavatories at the bottom of the yard, gaslights. Nearby was a canal with
a footbridge. The water was opaquely grey, laced with
effluent from factories and mills so that it appeared to
be oily; sometimes I would see a sleekly glistening
water-rat move along the cobblestoned embankment.
Children used to kick at the cobblestones with clogs,
so that the glancing blows would strike showers of
sparks from their irons. On Sundays all but the most
grimly atheistic would dress in their best suits, coats,
hats, shoes and go to church, the Protestants heading

in one direction, the Catholics in another. Often our paths crossed at the bridge. We passed each other, nodding warily for, although we would be neighbours or friends for the rest of the week, on days such as this we wore our differences like a uniform, and each group became antagonistic and proud with their sense of belonging. Inside the church I would sit with my parents on a hard pew of polished wood. I would stare at the back of the pew in front of us, or at the nearest support column, and sometimes at the minister as he preached an impenetrable and patronising sermon.

But I always enjoyed the hymns, and revelled in their confidence and vision. Their sonorous, ascendant cadences seemed to me to contain all the elements of belief – strength, direction, an harmonious completion. It was not until much later that the words began to ring with complacency and bombast. Until then, I sang with all the power of my lungs, certain that there had indeed been a Christ as clearly realisable as the figure in the frontispieces of children's bibles, and that there was without question a kind and omnipotent God who oversaw what everyone on earth did, thought, felt. I could lift up my eyes to where the holy spirit flared golden in the stained glass, and it did not strike me as at all unlikely that, one day, the clouds would part and glory, divinity and truth would walk again upon the earth.

4

I COULD TELL WHO THEY WERE AS SOON AS THEY GOT OFF THE TRAIN. I had arrived early, so early that I was worried that the time limit would have expired on the car park by the time I returned to it. I walked up and down the echoing platform. Even though the sun turned the high glass into sheets of brilliance, there was still a chill. When I finally saw the train heading down the long curve of track towards the station mouth I felt curiously lightheaded, as if I had breathed pure oxygen.

They looked slighter, and more pale, than their photographs. They stepped carefully from the carriage, and did not look up at the girders and columns as new arrivals often do. Such surroundings were, perhaps, already familiar to them.

They were both dressed casually. Croft wore a shirt and loose trousers the colour of pale sand, with an unzipped green weatherproof jacket. His hair was fairer than I had expected, but cropped close to the skull; above the temples, it was thin. On his chin was a day or so's growth of stubble. After his time in Australia I had expected him to be tanned, but he had a convict's pallor. An airline bag was slung over one shoulder. I could not help but notice that his body had no excess fat at all, and that his eyes had the unblinking stoicism of a man who has spent much of his time alone with himself.

The girl was even more different from how I had imagined her. Her black hair had been fashionably cut to show the nape of her neck. Her eyes, set in a pale oval face, were quite startling. She appeared cautious, possibly unhappy, and clasped her bag in front of herself. Her clothes, although functional, were stylish, down to the white leather shoes. Apart from the Oriental cast to her face she could have been one of the many girls of her age I had seen in town.

We introduced ourselves and shook hands. Until recently I had never done any manual work, so my hands were small. Kim's, in mine, felt tiny and crushable, but Croft's grip was that of an athlete.

Their bags were light, as if filled with only one change of clothes; I loaded them into the boot and we set off. At first, unsure what to say, I asked about their journey. Neither seemed eager to talk; when they did, it was in short sentences which did not invite a reply. Kim's voice, although recognisably American, was not overpoweringly so, and I could detect no trace of any Vietnamese accent.

I drove past the brewery, the biscuit factory, the sorting office, and out through the suburbs. I explained that they would have been able to reach me by taking the coastal train, but that it would take a long time and the connections were not good. Neither of them thanked me for having met them at the station. Made a little nervous by their taciturn presence, I began to indicate some local landmarks – the church with its graveyard shaped like a playing-card because it was built on Roman foundations, the partial remains of a Norman castle, the long line of pit cottages at the top of a rise, the barren slagbank that was being carted away in a convoy of lorries.

'And after the Romans and the Normans,' Croft said, 'you had no more invaders, just refugees. Huguenots, European Jews, Hungarians, Ugandan Asians, Vietnamese.'

I was surprised he could quote such a list. 'Not many of them really, Mr Croft. Not in this part of the country.'

'The Thucs, Maurice; when do I get to see the Thucs?' He accented the last syllable, so that in his mouth my name became oddly misshapen.

I glanced in the mirror and saw Kim looking at me with wide eyes, but she immediately looked away. 'I don't know, Mr Croft. I'm in something of a dilemma. Perhaps I should have been more stubborn with you when I told you not to come.'

'They have to see me, and they will do.'

'You have no grounds for such confidence.'

'I'll find them. You needn't take me. You can refuse if that would help your conscience.'

'I'm not refusing, not yet. But neither can I particularly help you just yet. We need to know a little more about each other.'

'We?'

'I'm interested in you, Mr Croft. I would appreciate knowing more about you. Tonight I hope we'll all get to know each other a little better.'

There was a pause, then he said, 'Maurice, it's not that I don't appreciate your hospitality, because I do – but what makes you think I want to know more about you?'

I found the question brutal, and it stung me. I tried to ignore it. 'You need a middleman – isn't that the phrase? I suspect you know it yourself. After all, you wrote to the *News* and you phoned me. It's almost as if the Thucs were presenting you with a special problem. Is that true? I used to know them well, although I've only seen them once over the past few years. That was when I tried to get them to help you.'

'Tell me about the family.'

'You're trying to pump me for information.'

I had to stop at traffic lights beside some roadworks, and looked sideways at Croft. He had one hand up to his mouth, and was running his fingers along his lower lip. Only then did I notice that his nails were bitten to the quick.

We were through the lights before he spoke again. 'We can't really spend too much time playing games, Maurice. Kim and me, we want this thing to be over.'

Once more I caught her looking at me through the mirror; once more, she darted her gaze away. 'It may take longer than you would like. Perhaps the Thucs would respond to a different strategy. It might be helpful, for instance, if you told them, and me, all that you know.'

'You know,' he said with heavy irony, 'when I was a kid I used to go to movies where there was always a priest, a Karl Malden type, who wanted to be part of the action. He always had to prove himself a regular guy, always had to get things sorted out. Most of all he always wanted to *understand* people.'

'Are we nearly there?' Kim asked suddenly.

I pointed ahead, beyond the embankment. 'Once through that arch we'll see the sea.'

Fifteen minutes later we were at the cottage. I unlocked the door and let them in. It was not until they entered that I felt, for the first time in months, that the cottage was instantly identifiable as belonging to someone who was solitary, aging, with all his life behind him. It lacked the touch of a second person. Perhaps I should have accepted Celia's offers to redecorate the rooms, spruce them up. Stubbornly, I had refused her several times.

I explained that there were only two bedrooms; the one I used, and a spare. My own looked out over the reserve, and had a window I had meant to fix for several months. Only that morning I had noticed that a ribbon of moss was forcing the dried putty away from the glass. Inside the room was my own bed, which was covered with a multicoloured blanket woven by Peruvian Indians. I had bought it not because I liked it, but because I expected it of myself to show sympathy and solidarity with the Third World, no matter how small. Merely buying it made some kind of point about the inequality of wealth, although I suspected that the weavers themselves would get about a hundredth of its European price. I had grown attached to it, nevertheless, and kept it folded across the bottom of the bed even in summer, when it was not needed. Its repeated patterns of bright primary colours gave the room a warmth it would not otherwise have had. Above the bed-head, directly above so that it could not be seen from the pillow, was a plain wooden cross. At first I had placed it on the opposite wall, but I had disliked it even there. Its very simplicity was ostentatious, like a statement of high uncluttered ideals. I had had to move it. In the room, too, was an old dressing-table, late forties style. We had been given it as a wedding present. It was one of the few things that remained from the early days of my marriage. Like a good husband and father,

I still had photographs of my wife and Jessica placed on it, but, thinking that perhaps Kim would take my bed, I had folded these and put them in one of the drawers. I did not wish either her or Croft to think that they had been put there specially for them.

To one side of the dressing-table were my shelves of books. My natural history books, my local histories, were kept in the living-room, along with the last Crockford's I had bought. Those in my bedroom were mostly paperbacks, bought on recommendation or impulse. I had looked at all the spines just in case there could have been something to which Kim might take exception. There was nothing.

The spare room was barer, even Spartan. There was a double-bed, a few closed packing-cases, and that was all. The carpet did not even fully cover the floorboards. The bed was about forty years old; my marriage bed. We had enough sheets, blankets, eiderdowns given to us to last a lifetime. Those on it had scarcely been used. I had aired them especially for the Crofts, for it was a long time since anyone had stayed with me. The packing cases held the remnants of my former life – letters, official documents, theology books. I never looked at them but had not been able to throw them away. None of them were important. My will, my bank statements, my insurances, my keys were all kept in the living-room.

There was some discussion as to where we should sleep. I told them I had changed the sheets; I feared that my widower's clutter would make them think that the place was unclean. There was a disagreement, surprisingly good-natured, and in the end I accepted Croft's scheme – Kim would use the spare room and he would sleep on the couch in front of the fire. Even though it was still only late afternoon, I explained where everything was – the light switches, in case they woke in the night and were uncertain where they were (although I told them there would be light in the sky until after eleven, and the dawn would begin not too long after that), the lavatory (I was worried that Kim, used to American sanitation, would find it too basic, with its whitewashed walls and rusting chrome toilet-paper holder screwed into the wall), the bathroom (again, I was aware of the ugliness of the taps, and how there was a stain the colour of urine beneath the hot one, and how the enamel was veined with hairline cracks).

I made a meal. I was unsure what to prepare, since I did not know what they would be used to eating. In the end I had bought a kind of cheese pie from a supermarket in town, because I thought they might be vegetarians. When I asked if that would be all right, Croft nodded absentmindedly and walked outside. A few seconds later he passed the window, gazing upwards as if he were surveying the building.

'He checks out everything,' Kim said. 'You shouldn't be offended.'

I thought of Croft creeping through jungle undergrowth among diagonal slats of light. 'He'll not go too far away, will he?'

'Not yet. He'll stick close.'

I began to cook some extra vegetables. I was feeling obscurely guilty. I had led Croft to believe that there was more hope with the Thucs than I actually believed possible. Even if he did get to meet them the whole of his journey would have been wasted. I had misled someone who was the nearest thing to a hero I would ever meet, and I had done that because of my own selfishness. Despite my reservations, I had wanted to come face to face with a kind of nobility. In Luciano Croft I could recognise it. I could even forgive his strange manners and his brusqueness.

'You call him your father?' I asked.

'I used to call him Pop – can you imagine that? Dad was the next stage on. It used to seem better when we were in England, anyway. Now I call him Lucky.'

I was surprised. 'You've been to England before?'

'Sure. Didn't you know?'

I shook my head.

'We were here, oh, a couple of years, almost. This was where she was killed.'

'Mrs Croft?'

'A car. She was the driver. It was no one else's fault. She went into the back of a truck. Lucky says she broke her neck straight away. She didn't suffer.'

She had been too young to die, I thought. I had believed that about my own wife too, even though I had seen people die who were much younger than either of them. The Edmondson girl had scarcely been of school age when she had wandered away from her parents and somehow fallen into the river. Hours later, she had been discovered downstream. I often thought of her when I came across the bones of livestock on the estuary. It was the same river.

There was the click of an opening door. 'I thought you'd gone,' I said cheerily.

'It's a tiny place you've got. Isolated. You must be pleased to have that phone.'

'I don't use it that much,' I said.

'Emergencies?'

'I don't have any.'

The meal was acceptable but not exceptional. Before he ate, Croft picked up his knife and fork and examined each, testing the edges and prongs with his thumb. I glanced at Kim, but she did not look up. Perhaps it was customary for Americans to do this.

I had to prompt conversation several times. Croft appeared to have so much on his mind that he could take only a cursory interest in what was going on. Fortunately, Kim could be encouraged into talking about the places they had visited. Her descriptions were mixtures of worldweariness and enthusiasm. Often she talked as if she knew nothing about the places at all, and I wondered how much she had been able to see of New York, Washington, Hong Kong, Singapore, Paris, Lyons, Auckland, Melbourne, Sydney. All the time Croft said nothing, although he continued to eat methodically and waste nothing.

'And England?' I asked.

Croft, realising I was talking specifically to him, looked at me with a disconcertingly unblinking stare.

I cleared my throat. 'I heard you spent some time in England a while ago.'

'A few years back,' he replied. 'My wife was killed in London. We took her ashes back home and I poured them out in a field and dug them into the earth. After that Kim and me started to travel.'

I began to sympathise, but he interrupted.

'Don't say you're sorry, Maurice. It was meant to be. You don't think this is romantic, do you, all this stuff you've been asking Kim to talk about? You don't sit there and envy our life of departure lounges and waiting rooms and grimy trains and dead ends? Kim's no age to travel. The best years of your life are spent in one place, as a child. Only when you're eighteen, nineteen should you tear yourself away. We live our lives on charity, hustling for free beds and meals, just like I hustled you. I spend my days in public records offices, checking up old clippings, watching old newsreels. Everything boils down to a jumble, a ragbag, a stew. I'll be pleased when it's finished.'

'But you don't know when that will be.'

'No.'

'Which is where the Thucs come in.'

'You got it. Let me show you something.' He got up and went for his bag, which had been left in one corner of the room. From it he drew a plastic cylinder almost two feet long, which he uncapped. Inside was a piece of paper rolled up like a map. When he unrolled part of it I could see that it was covered with names, addresses, phone numbers that had been boxed, interlinked, cross-referenced. 'Not just a straight family tree,' he explained, 'but also a grouping of contacts, neighbours, friends all over the globe.' He pointed to one place on its surface. There were the names, but not the address, of the Thucs. Several thin lines, far more tentative than most of the others, led from them to other parts of the chart.

'It's wrong,' I said.

He looked at me, but did not appear astonished, as I had hoped.

'There are two children down there, and there's only one, Ky. It must be a different family.'

'The other son died on the boat. Didn't they tell you that?'

'No,' I said, abashed. Then, trying to recover my position, I added, 'Or I may have forgotten.'

He smiled as he rolled up the sheet and pushed it back into its holder. 'They're the ones all right. They're the answer.'

Later I took them on a short walk across the reserve. The cottage was becoming unusually claustrophobic, even though Kim had gone into the spare room and lain on the bed with a tape machine beside her and earphones on her head, even though Croft had sat outside and entered a long period of silence.

There had been calm, settled weather for more than a week now, although sometimes after dusk a wind, generated by the temperature gradients between land and water, scoured the dunes. At this hour of the day the sand was a riddle of old tracks, from the trampled areas where the gulls had landed to the delicate indentations, like stitchings, where solitary beetles had traversed the lee sides of mounds. In one small hollow I came across the droppings of a fox, crumbling into dust because they were old, pieces of bone showing within them. Like a proud parent showing off the works of his child, I walked the ridges and hollows pointing out what I thought were places of interest;

CHRISTOPHER BURNS

I told them anecdotally about the behaviour of gulls, the spread of sea buckthorn, the times when egg cases were cast up along the shore. I stopped at the flint bed, and said that although there was nothing to see now, apart from the occasional piece of knap, it was an important stage in the colonisation of the area six thousand or so years ago. 'More invaders,' Croft said laconically. I said that it was better seen as a slow domestication of a wild and uninhabited land. He smiled briefly.

I took them to the hut, unlocked it and showed them inside. Kim hung back, uninterested, but Croft looked round and nodded. I wondered if his knowledge of hides and camouflage was substantial; I could imagine him holed up in one, not moving for days.

Kim was disappointed that she could not walk in the sea. The tide was out, and there was half a mile or so of shining sand between her and the shallow, unhurried waves. I took her a short way along the beach to a rock pool, and Croft and I sat on the shingle while she took off her shoes, rolled up her jeans and walked into it, shrieking at the sudden cold. 'It'll feel warm soon,' I shouted. 'Careful or you'll soak your clothes. It'll be knee-deep.'

I turned to Croft, about to comment on her enjoyment, and saw that his eyes were shining as if they brimmed with tears. Almost immediately he stood up and walked away from me, sitting down again a few

72

yards further along the beach. I waited for a short while then followed him.

I put up a hand to indicate the entire area. 'This may not be as important as you hope,' I said gently. 'What could the Thucs tell you that you don't already know? Your name, and Kim's, mean nothing to them.'

'They're vital,' he said, refusing to look at me. Then suddenly he turned, his eyes a little red, but with his voice urgent and his expression ferocious. 'I'm closer than I've ever been. Don't you see a pattern to all this? We've returned after years of wandering to where the journey began. That must mean something. It's like hearing the tumblers click one by one as a safe-door is opened.'

'If you want to think that, Luciano,' I said guardedly. For me the world seemed built in a haphazard fashion, with no fateful thread running through it, the result of chance and necessity alone.

'Maurice, have you turned your back on God?'

I did not answer.

'He puts everyone to the test – you included. Our period of trial has been hard and long, but for others it's worse.'

I watched him as he picked up a handful of pebbles and looked at each one before letting it fall. I was fascinated by Croft's mission, but had never thought of it as being underpinned by any kind of religious belief. The word *God* surprised and faintly shocked me. I had wanted his altruism, his commitment to be both humane and humanist, a demonstration of ordinary, unmystical goodness. Now I began to wonder if a sense of religious duty lay at its root.

I cleared my throat. 'God?'

Now, having raised God, it seemed as though he wished to avoid the subject. 'Does that make you think you have something in common with me?' he asked harshly.

'No. Each of us draws whatever meaning we can from his own experience. Yours and mine are vastly different.'

'Damn right,' he said, speaking before I had finished.

I looked at Kim. She was just out of earshot, and had found a rock free of barnacles on which she sat, splashing her feet in the water. She looked much younger than her years now. 'Luciano, be honest with me. Did you know Kim's mother?'

For a moment I thought he would refuse to answer, but then he spoke. 'I'd never seen her before in my life. It was utter madness at that time. There was space for me on one of those Giants, always had been. But I was young and foolhardy, or so I thought then. I had a part to play, that was the real reason. I wanted to take things to the brink, to feel death snap at my heels. The Giant was overloaded when I tried to get on it. At the last minute, you better believe it, I was scared. I wanted to be out of that place.'

'They were coming closer?'

'I'd listened to them since the barrage on Tan Son Nhut airport. There was mortar fire away to the east, coming closer to the Embassy all the time. We had to chop down a tamarind to make sure there was enough space for the Giants to land. People had been locked outside the gates but were scrambling over the wall, and the marines had been on methedrine for so long that they didn't know what the hell to do for a lot of the time. We were cramming seventy people into Chinooks that were made for fifty, and as the firing got nearer and the panic began to grow, we were pushing in ninety. Up on the roof the incinerators weren't working properly, and all the money we'd decided to burn came floating down, half-charred. When it came to my turn everything seemed to have gone completely crazy, but I remember those few seconds as clear as day, as if they had only just happened. I hit the rim of the door scrambling up into it. Only later did I see that my knee was bleeding. Inside everyone was packed tighter than in any cattle-truck, some of them weeping, all of them overdosed on shock and relief and fear. A whole mass of other people were scrambling for the door, and inside some guy kept shouting that we should shoot them, shoot them, shoot them, because if they had hung onto the struts we would never have gotten away. I thought of those faces as a sea, and those hands as waves beating against a bulwark. As we lifted, the machine lurched because there was so much weight in it. I was at the very edge; some guy was struggling to close the door. I still couldn't believe that I had finally stepped onto the thing, and had a sensation of having been hit across the side of the head because I was lightheaded and dizzy. Then a woman lifted something up out of the crowd.'

We sat quietly. Beyond the dunes the evening train went up the line, the vibration of its passage changing notes as it travelled north.

'I knew straightaway that it was a child, little more than a baby. I reached out and didn't think about what I was doing. It was purely reflex, a response that someone makes when they're faced with anguish and pleading. I didn't think that we would connect, but something made us. Despite the roar that told me how the engine strained, despite the beat of the rotors, that machine just floated light as any feather for those few inches, making us come together so that I could take the child and pull her into my chest. Then we lifted as if guyropes had been cut, and the whole scene dropped, plummeted beneath us. The woman's hands disappeared into the crowd like someone vanishing beneath quicksand. They got the door closed and I was wedged up against it, and through it I could see the embassy gardens still crowded, the smoke, the streets. We tilted away and curved out toward the sea. I held Kim as safe as I could, cradling her to me. She was crying and I didn't know what to do, but I was drained, exalted, scared. Everything had changed, but I had no idea what I had done.'

'You had performed a selfless act during a time of great selfishness, Luciano.'

'You'd feel better if that was true, Maurice? I can't claim to have done anything like that. It was as involuntary as a knee-jerk.'

'That doesn't make it any less selfless, just as it doesn't mean that you're somehow less good. The important thing is that you acted. In a very literal sense, you're a saviour.'

He shook his head as Kim came walking towards us along the beach, her feet sinking into the damp sand. 'You did right to take her from her mother. There was no alternative.'

'Mother? She could have been anyone – sister, aunt, friend.'

Kim had found a swell of sand that was so soft that she sank over her ankles in it, and was retracing her steps so the footprints deepened. 'You didn't want to trace her until after your wife died?' I asked.

'It was in my mind, and I did nothing about it even though it worried at me like an ache. That crash made it all clear to me. I had spent years denying my purpose. When she was killed, I knew that I had been given a warning.'

'I don't understand.'

'God punishes those who refuse him. I had delayed too long; my term had begun.'

I felt a shiver of unease. I had come to accept that death was capricious and purposeless; now Croft, of all people, was telling me that he believed in a God who would destroy the innocent just to precipitate a course of action. 'Surely not,' I said, astonished at the Old Testament barbarity of his vision.

'You belong to a kind of eunuch religion, Maurice. No offence, but you do. You live such blinkered lives you can't see what goes on in the world.'

'Luciano, all of us try to make patterns of our lives. It's a natural instinct, and no one could blame you for that. You've taken on the most demanding of tasks; you're a good man unable to give up. That's all there is to it. There's no need to involve the divine.'

'Ignore the evidence, you mean? God is so real you could almost touch him. He's here now. Can't you sense him?'

It was an ordinary day, with nothing special about it at all.

'I don't think I'd recognise your God,' I said after a while. 'He's too brutal. And too mercenary.'

'Terms, labels – those are modern things, humanist things. Abraham wouldn't have said that. He would have slit that boy's throat if he'd had to.'

'A myth, that's all. And Abraham would have been criminally insane if he'd done that.'

'The Greeks saw patterns, didn't they? Patterns that still disturb us. Murder, incest, sacrifice. And they were a high civilisation, so I hear.'

'This is far too simple. You can't think of God in these terms. Theology – '

He interrupted me. 'Theology? Your ancestors squatting back there on the flint bed would have had a better idea of theology. Gathered round a fire on a dark and stormy night, surrounded by wolves and the unknown and terrible mystery, they would be able to recognise more than you could – and probably me as well. God puts us on a rack, Maurice. He gets pleasure from seeing us suffer. He divides, he joins together, he engineers betrayal. He makes us all betray. There's no such thing as heroism, and the good you speak of is like a little light that flickers in a dark forest at night, then dies.'

'The just causes are the heaviest to take up,' I countered, 'and I can well believe that the courageous are the last to see their own virtue.'

Kim came walking up the shingle, her shoes in her hands. Once or twice, when she stood on a sharp stone, she teetered but she never lost her balance. I looked at the damp prints of her soles, turned into abstract geometries by the curvatures of the pebbles.

'Enjoy it?' I asked, and she nodded quickly. She seemed full of life.

We walked back across the reserve with the sun sinking towards the sea, turning it into a blaze of light. As we walked our shadows strode before us across the hummocks of marram and sand.

Back inside the cottage Kim said she wanted to have a bath. Croft and I sat together and listened to the water hammer in the pipes and the cistern refill. When she had finished Kim came to thank me for the use of the room, then went to bed. For a while we heard her portable hairdryer, then the distant tinny sound of music.

'Tomorrow,' I said, 'we'll drive to town. I'll see if I can persuade the Thucs to see you.'

I had expected him to be grateful, but he did not reply for a while. When he did, he merely said, 'I'll go on my own.'

'You can't. I wouldn't let you.'

He smiled without humour, and pointed to Kim's room. 'Hear that music? She listens to the same things over and over again.'

'You would do the same at her age.'

'I listened to most of my music in the streets and brothels of Saigon. The girls used to perform to all that sixties stuff. Do I shock you?'

'I think you may be trying to.'

'Listen, I've done things in my life you'd not like to know about. It was a pleasure palace, that city, able to give the most outrageous gifts. So long as the dollars were there, so long as death underscored it all, then all the delights of life, all its degradations, were just as easy as reaching out and picking an apple off a tree. I took some of those things. I'm a corrupted man, weak and treacherous.'

'Are you trying to make me think less of you? I'm not in the business of judging my fellow men.' Although I did not say it, I was thinking that many of the most holy and inflexible of saints had led lives of sensuality and violence before their conversions.

'I'm telling you that Kim may have come from that sort of world.'

'Maybe. But you wouldn't return her to someone who would do her harm.'

'Why not? The harm may be less than she's getting now. I do what I have to do, that's all. I'm a pawn in the game, even if everyone wants me to be something else. To some I'm a knight in shining armour, to others a scapegoat, a man bound to history because of a kind of moral lottery. Some think

I'm expiating the sins of a nation. Others that I'm exorcising an individual guilt. Do you want a different Lucky Croft, Maurice? What kind of features would you draw on my face? Not a saint's or an angel's – I've warned you about that.'

'I suppose I'd try to draw the real you.'

'You sound like a cheap journalist looking for a snappy line. You disappoint me, I guess. And yet we have certain things in common, don't we? A certain isolation, maybe. All those envelopes over there – your daughter?'

All of a sudden I was annoyed at Croft, and achingly jealous of him. All of his time was consumed by his quest. He had a target, a goal, and therefore there was about his life the chance of completeness. 'You have Kim, don't you?' I asked angrily. 'Do you really want to return her to a network of relations who may not care about her, who may want to turn their backs on the past? Does it make you feel good to think of yourself as the all-American loner, like all those heroes you saw in the cinema as a kid? Why do you want rid of her – surely you must care for her, surely you must love her?'

Even as I spoke I was thinking of Jessica, all those miles away, and of my constantly deferred decision to stop writing to her.

'Love?' he replied, with sudden scorn. 'You have the audacity to talk to me about love?'

I took away my gaze and looked into the fire. It was true, I thought; his was a selfless love. I had no right to question it.

We were silent for a while then, quietly, he mentioned the Thucs again.

'I was waiting for you to come back to them,' I said.

'I met a woman in Australia. She was one of the Cholon Chinese who came out of Vietnam in the late seventies. She came first to Malaysia by boat, and then on to Sydney. She'd known a lot of people in Saigon because she called herself a doctor – not a Western doctor, but a herbalist, a wise woman. A lot of people swore by her medicines and said how good she was. She had a file full of testimonials from people she'd made love potions for, or charms to ward off the evil eye. She said she never threw any of them away because she was scared the Australians might investigate her some day.'

'She still worked?'

'No kidding, getting out of Vietnam was the best thing that ever happened to her. She was making herself rich by exporting stuff to the States; she was even talking about settling there, although I guess she may have had trouble with some of the constituents she used. The Occident has a touching faith in Oriental wisdom. Anyhow, I showed her the photographs. Said she knew the woman.'

I felt a quiver of apprehension. 'And?'

'She didn't know her name, couldn't tell me where she was, didn't even know where she'd seen her.'

'She's not Mrs Thuc. I can tell you that.'

'I begged her to tell me more, but she wouldn't. Then she told me that many of her customers asked about relatives and friends, and if they sent donations she could maybe help. Donations was her word – she'd already picked up the right way of talking about money. So they sent their donation and some little item, like a piece of clothing, a toy, a lock of hair, and she did what she could. I asked if she could do something with the photographs and whatever money I could give her. At first she said no, and I could tell that she knew I was desperate so she was holding out for more. She made me wait. In the end I'd have got down and kissed that little gook's feet if she'd told me to. I probably paid her a damn sight more cash than most of her other clients. She said she needed it to go to California.'

'And?'

'She bolted the doors, lowered the lights, bound my wrists together with a white cloth, and started muttering to herself. I thought she was taking me, but then there was this God-awful noise from out of her throat, rasping and loud, so loud I didn't believe it could come from such a little woman. After that she started talking in English, with a bit of French thrown in, and sometimes a little of her own language.' He paused for a while before continuing. 'She told me she was being shown a family who moved north, among cold weather and rain and beside a sea, a grey sea.'

'That could be anywhere.'

'She pointed it out on a map I put on the table in front of her. She didn't know which country it was, but her fingernail touched exactly where we are now.'

'Coincidence.'

'She said there had been two children, both boys, but one died when they were becalmed in the middle of an ocean. He'd been too weak to begin with. The other son lived, and was interested in a place that was like a desert, but which had grass growing along ridges of sand and lots of birds in the sky that made a constant noise.'

'That doesn't fit. Not anymore.'

'It used to, though, didn't it? She told me their name as well. Thuc.'

'Perhaps that's a common name. And probably she knew it anyway, and was setting you up. They all came out at the same time, didn't they? They could even have been on the same boat.'

'Thuc had a sister. He made a living on the black market, selling goods he had lifted from American stores. His sister was a bar-girl. She had a daughter called Phuong; it means phoenix. It all fits. She rose out of the ashes that day I reached out and lifted her up.'

'It *was* the mother, then?'

He was silent.

'But you don't know that. You don't know anything for sure. Luciano, it seems likely that your woman just told you what she knew you wanted to hear. Clairvoyants make a living out of doing that. She knew a little, embroidered it – either that or, without you knowing it, she drew information out of you and built it into an elaborate fiction. Whatever the case, the central point is that the Thucs recognise no one in your photographs.'

'You were there when they saw them?'

'Part of the time.'

'What do you mean – you were either there or you weren't.'

I had a sense of wandering into a dark shadow. 'I was there, but not when Mr Thuc saw them.'

'The grandmother?'

'She'd gone into the kitchen.'

'Deliberately?'

'I suppose so. She must have been cooking or cleaning – I don't know. Does it matter?'

'The son's too young, but the mother must have known. When you handed them over, what did Mrs Thuc's face look like? Was there an instant, a split-second maybe, when her true feelings showed?

Something that would make you realise if she was lying afterwards?'

I said nothing. At that crucial moment I had looked away.

5

MY MIND WAS TOO ACTIVE, and for a long time I could not sleep. Instead my imagination conjured scenes of meetings between Croft, Kim and the Thucs – scenes which were contradictory and jostled each other for precedence, fictions in which the characters showed shock, embarrassment, joy, rage, indifference. I could not bring these inventions fully to life. Each action, each speech was stilted and unreal, as if delivered by amateur actors. I imagined, too, that each of these people would confidently explain his or her feelings, rather than keep them hidden. Nevertheless, I returned to such fantasies like an obsessive, as if their stunted development and insane reiteration would finally enable my mind to rest.

Eventually, and without knowing it, I fell asleep. And woke up with a start, not knowing what the time was. All around me the room was strange, as if the perspectives had shifted in the darkness. I had the impression that outside a light had just been switched off. The sense of disorientation was so acute that I sat up rapidly, making spots of livid colour swirl within my field of vision. Some years before I had suffered from mild blood pressure; I forced myself to sit quietly and calmed myself by breathing regularly and deeply. A sense of place and time began to restore itself. I placed my bare feet on the reassuring flock of the carpet, moving them back and forward. The room's shadowings and pale washes of grey light once more became familiar to me. After a while I could stand up, but I held out my hands like a tight-rope walker for fear that I would be seized by vertigo, lose balance, and fall.

The living-room was grey, its forms merged but for the dull red of the dying fire, only just visible as a fading grid around the ash. On the sofa was a shapeless heap, beneath which Croft was sleeping.

As quietly as I could I walked to the lavatory. There was little illumination coming through the frosted glass, so I switched on the light. I felt old, tired, and weak. I stood over the bowl with my shoulders hunched; it took me half a minute or so before I could begin to urinate. When I did the smell was sharp and unpleasant, as if I had been ill. Afterwards the cistern clanked and refilled with a prolonged sibilant hiss. I closed the door on it and padded back through the living-room, hands still outstretched.

'Goodnight, Maurice.'

Croft's voice was clear and unsleepy, but I could not see his face.

I replied without thinking – 'Goodnight, Luciano.' I was surprised that he was so alert.

I got back into bed and curled up, feeling slightly unwell. And I remembered, across more than fifty years, getting better after a childhood illness and yet feeling drowsily, pleasantly weakened. My mother said I needn't go to school for a couple of days. I stayed in bed, getting out only to use the lavatory, and she brought me meals on trays while I stayed snug beneath the blankets and read the comics that my father bought for me. I was protected from the world, and had never been so happy.

I had loved my parents then, and the comfort they had given me had been foremost in my mind when Jessica suffered a childhood illness. My wife and I provided for her and pampered her as much as we could; I brought her extra presents and always made time to sit on the edge of the bed and talk to her, or join in with her word games. I was already uncomfortably aware that, as we age, illness becomes a condition which we have to face alone.

I had been helpless during the deaths of my parents and, later, my wife. I watched as disease devoured her, making her less and less like the person who had shared my life. Once the diagnosis was established, this could not be a surprise. I had witnessed hundreds of similar cases. Relatives had called me out to be a comfort to someone close to them who was dying. I had developed the experience to deal with them efficiently. In rooms that smelled of perfumes, liberally sprinkled to cover the smell of bodily collapse, I would grasp the hands of those who would die soon. I could be lugubriously solemn or chirpily ebullient, gauging what was needed by the reactions of my audience. Always I would be ready with sympathy, a prayer, a few comforting verses about eternity, heaven, resurrection. With my own wife I was unequal to the task.

I loved her; there had never been any doubt about that. And yet this love was like a barrier which prevented me from helping her. We had been honest with each other, and I could not comfort her without being dishonest. At the time, Jessica was living away, but she came back to be with her mother at the end. I was impressed by Jessica, and felt unequal to her candour. My wife seemed to appreciate such a forthright daughter; my own attempts at help were, by comparison, stunted and ill-timed.

Often I wondered if this experience had left a lasting mark on Jessica. Certainly since that time she had begun to treat me as someone who was well-meaning but misguided. She began, too, to send me little booklets on Eastern mysticism which I found to be arcane, indulgent and top-heavy with metaphor and symbol. I never tried to read them seriously.

I could not stop her marriage, and would not have dared to try, although I knew that it was foolish. He was a kind, well-meaning man, but a little too staid and too unimaginative for Jessica. I had the sense that she felt she was marrying below herself, although she never expressed this. When the children were born, however, I came to believe that their family would stay together. I was shocked when Jessica decided that it should not. There were no great problems, she explained to me, it was just that she and her husband were obviously unsuited to each other; much better to do something about it now rather than later. When I demurred, and suggested there was no reason why they should not stay together, she looked at me incredulously. They had discovered the fault; why spend the rest of their lives in frustration and unease?

She pursued the divorce with speed and single-mindedness, and never asked me for advice or guidance. Instead, she chose to read sections from texts which I thought at best absurd, at worst fakes. When it was all over, she told me that from her settlement, and from money she had earned, she had enough to go to live in India with the children. They could survive frugally, she said. But the main reason for their departure was that she wanted to experience directly what she had only read about. There was a holy man, a teacher, who lived in a kind of communal village; his name had been given to her, and she had already paid for six months' stay, although it was likely that she would stay longer. I knew that she would stay indefinitely if she could, but I would not beg her not to go. Before the plane took off I told her that this was a dangerous, possibly catastrophic thing to do, and I hugged her, and my grandchildren, one last time.

From the first letter onwards, every thing was upbeat, everything was going her way. An American called Rick had shown her round and looked after Amanda when she had fallen and cut her knee. Jessica had made the right decision, she told me; there was no doubt that she was on the upward path. I sat with her letter, full of ridiculous mystifications, and felt that I had been deserted.

It was just after six when I woke up, although I felt I had slept neither long nor deeply enough. My eyes were sore and there was a sour, stale taste in my mouth. I lay in bed for a few minutes, listening to the sound of birds. Two gulls squabbled on the roof, making a series of flurrying thumps as they hopped across the slates. There was no noise from the other rooms.

Eventually I got up and dressed methodically, taking my time about it. If Croft was still asleep I would tiptoe past him, leave a short note saying

I would be back in an hour, and walk across the dunes. When I opened the door, however, I saw that the sofa was empty, and that the blanket had been folded with a military exactitude and left square on one of the cushions. I expected him to be in the lavatory or bathroom, but, when after several minutes there was no sound from either, I gave each door an experimental shove. They were both empty.

Then I thought he must be outside, but there was no sign of him. The air was bright and clear, with no cloud at all, and I seemed to be the only person awake for miles.

A fear, only partly formulated, came into my mind; I went back inside and stood at the door of the spare room. I could hear nothing. I put my hand on the jambs and tilted my body forward, angling my head so that I could hear better. Nothing. I stood back, wondering what to do, then went into the kitchen. After I had put on the kettle I was still nervous, still like a man hesitating before making an unpleasant but necessary decision. Finally I went back to the door and spoke Kim's name so that it would be heard inside her room. There was no reply.

I put my fingers on the door and gave it the lightest of pushes. At the second attempt, marginally stronger than the first, it gave. I had noticed its creak before, but never that it was so loud. When the gap was large enough for me to put my head and shoulders through, I did so, peering round it like an intruder and ready to draw back quickly. Kim lay asleep, breathing lightly. Strands of her hair lay in glossy black trails on the pillow. I eased myself back out of the room and clicked the door shut behind me.

I made myself a coffee and sat looking out of the window. Five minutes later I went back outside, crossed the silent road, and stood by the fence that marked the perimeter of the reserve. I looked near the fence to see if I could see the imprint of his shoes, but the only tracks were from the day before. Even though I scanned the dunes through my binoculars, I could see no sign of Croft.

'Kim?' I asked, standing at the closed door of her bedroom.

'What's that?' she asked, muffled and lazy.

'Did Luciano say what he was going to do this morning?'

The reply was indistinct.

'I think he must have gone onto the reserve. Would he do that?'

The door opened. She stood behind it in a teeshirt and, it appeared, very little else. One hand was in her hair, and her eyes were bruised by sleep. Disturbingly, she resembled certain photographs I had seen from the war – photographs of the bar girls of Saigon. I looked away quickly.

She yawned; I could feel the warmth of her breath as she exhaled. 'I wouldn't worry,' she said, 'he'll not be lost.'

I nodded as if I had accepted what she had to say; when I looked back at her she made a face as if there was nothing else to say. I turned away and she closed the door.

At that moment I remembered that, in the room where he had slept, I had left the keys to my car. Not only that, but my address book was in the top drawer of the sideboard, exactly where someone searching would look for it. It only took a short walk to my garage for my suspicions to be confirmed.

I telephoned Celia. She answered like a woman used to getting phone calls over breakfast. I told her that, although Kim was still here, Croft had vanished with my car.

'What do you mean, with your car? If you're saying he's stolen it, you should phone the police. Have you?'

'No. I said he should treat my cottage as his home. I didn't expect him to take me literally.'

I knew that she would be smiling in that mocking way that she had. 'Then you didn't really mean what you told him?'

I did not know whether to be abashed or annoyed. 'Perhaps the Americans are a literal people. But this isn't anything that should be reported to the police. The problem is – well, domestic.'

'Are you trying to tell me, Maurice, that he's on his way to the Thucs?'

'I think so, yes.'

I could hear her breath in the earpiece. 'Will he be there by now?'

'I didn't tell him the address. He must have looked it up.'

'In what?'

'My address book was with my car keys.'

'God, Maurice, why do you tempt people all the time?'

'Tempt? I don't do that.'

'Of course you do. You invite them to use you. You're like some kind of theological masochist waiting for the world to exercise its worst in front of you. It's like leaving money in a gutter and calling men thieves if they pick it up. What did you expect him to do? You act as if you're surprised, just like you acted surprised when the Edmondsons wanted the parish taken away from you. And now you're marooned with the girl, are you, with no way of getting out?'

'There's the train, but the next one's not until mid-day. And the Thucs aren't on the phone.'

'I'm going round there. Now.'

'Do you know where they live?'

'I know where *everyone* lives. It's my job. You'd better tell me what Croft told you about them. Quickly – I have to go now.'

I explained about Croft's visit to the clairvoyant, and how he was pinning all his hopes on the Thucs.

'This is lunatic,' Celia said when I'd finished; 'he has no evidence at all.'

'I suppose it's a chance,' I said defensively, 'perhaps even his last one.'

'Only the desperate would clutch at a straw like this one,' she replied drily. 'Your friend sounds like a textbook obsessive to me. I wouldn't like to cross him.'

'Whatever you say,' I replied. But I was thinking that I had never been in a position like Croft's. If there was a God, he had never chosen me, unless all the despair and the fleeting joys I had found during my ministry had been tests which, unknowingly, I had failed. 'What are you going to do, Celia?' I asked, although I knew I should have been telling her.

'I'm a reporter. I don't have any other function.'

'But you may not be able to remain a mere observer in this.'

'I'm practised in doing just that, Maurice. I'll contact you as soon as I can. If he turns up before I get back to you, hold on to him – I don't want him to give you the slip again. All right?'

I hung up feeling edgy and despondent. I had anticipated being there. I had thought that I would see the Thucs, reason with them, paint a picture of Croft's plight that was so vivid, so moving that they would have to capitulate. Then I would watch the truth unfold, layer by layer like a parcel being opened, and at last find out what lay at its heart. Now, however, I knew that I had been left on the periphery, waiting for people over whom I had no control.

When Kim reappeared her prettiness was more delicate, even fragile; she seemed the kind who could lose her beauty while only a young woman. I spoke her name with a forced jollity, as if this was our first meeting of the day and nothing was troubling my mind.

'You make early morning phone calls,' she said.

'You heard?'

'Bits.' She gave a tiny smile, fleeting but knowing. 'At times he just goes away. It's nothing to worry about. He'll be back.'

I shrugged. It was not an action I made often.

'He has a lot on his mind, so he'll be thinking things through. Making decisions.'

'Such as whether to pry in my personal files, take my car without permission, force himself on people who've expressly said they have no wish to see him?' Instantly, I regretted what I had said. 'I'm sorry, Kim; it's unfair to take it out on you.'

'It's all right.'

I had an unresolved bitterness within me, unable to take a direction. 'A man like me should know better – that's the irony. Of all of us, you are the only one who is truly innocent.'

She put her hands over her face. For several seconds I thought she was crying, and felt guiltily petty. Hesitantly, I reached out and put my arm round her shoulders. She flinched wildly, as if I had given her an electric shock, and I snatched my arm away. My wrist tingled, and I wondered if I had caught it on the chair back, so I half-nursed, half-rubbed it as I made my way back into the kitchen. I wished I could say something; I wished I had not renounced the facile sympathy which priests must use so fluently.

I could not understand why she had reacted in such a way. When I went back into the room, she was sitting motionless in the chair and her eyes had a bruised look. I decided to take a short walk down the road, certain that I would meet Croft returning with my car.

Just down from the cottage was the railway bridge. I stood within its bar of shadow, next to a sandstone abutment. Swifts, which nested in the girders, scythed through the air nearby. The river ran sluggishly at its summer level, the water pocked with bubbles of foam. High up on the banks, almost at the road's edge, were broken lines of twigs, dried black seaweed, a few bottletops, a doll's pink arm, all scattered along the sandy mud by a high tide which had bored up the river's mouth. Here, too, were the ribs and backbone of a sheep which had been carried downstream by a winter flood and then dumped. Only a few skeins of wool, gummed together, still remained.

The road was already beginning to swelter in the heat, and tar bubbles broke on its surface like fluid seeping through a bandage, There were sheep in a far field, almost motionless, cropping round a pylon; nearer there were Freisians and two Charolais, some lying down as if they reclined. Further, among the greens of grassland and hedge, there was wheat in its harvest colour and, slapped among them like a patch, a livid yellow field of rape. I began to realise that I wanted neither Croft nor Celia to arrive. If my own car was found, abandoned but unharmed, I would be content. I even wanted Kim to leave, to somehow disappear as if she had never existed. I wanted to be rid of all of them, to be left alone with my landscape, my animals, and the end of my life.

The sunshine made me drowsy; an insect droned in my ear. I could smell the cows, the rankness of the weeds by the bridge support, the heaviness of the hot tar. The passage of time sagged and lolled.

I had been there longer than I had intended, and was daydreaming when Celia drove along the road and pulled in just past the bridge, parking the car on the baked earth next to the entrance to the reserve. While I walked to meet her she opened the lid of the refuse bin I had had fitted next to the stile and dropped some old tickets into it. Despite her coolness, I could tell that she was flustered. 'The girl's still in there,' I said as soon as I was close enough.

'Not Croft?'

'No. No sign of him, either.'

The sunlight made her seem pale, and the lipstick looked too red. She pursed her mouth for a moment before she started to tell me what had happened. 'The Thucs are in an awful state. The wife looks as if she's been crying her eyes out, the old woman's just sitting in a corner rocking backward and forward as if she was in a trance, and Thuc himself is so agitated he looks as if he could be quite violent. He's supposed to go to work, but it would be as well if he didn't, not in that mood.'

I glanced across at the cottage to check if Kim was standing outside. 'What happened? Did they tell you?'

'The boy has the best English, but he's got out of the way. His father wasn't exactly easy to follow, but I think what happened is that Croft forced himself in, foot-in-the-door style. Once inside, he said that he had proof that Kim was their niece. They said he was wrong, that they had no niece. Croft produced the photographs again and said they were of Thuc's sister and a child named Phuong, and that they showed the child being handed to him when the embassy in Saigon was evacuated. He must have shown them the full shots. Thuc said he never had a sister, never had a niece. Croft called them liars. Things must have already been hopelessly strained and emotional, and somehow or other a fight, or more likely a scuffle, broke out. I noticed that a vase was broken, and the buttons on Thuc's shirt had been torn off.'

'And Croft?'

'This is what I don't understand. They seem to have been able to throw him out. You would have thought him difficult to move, wouldn't you? Anyway, out he went, and as soon as he was outside he collapsed on the grass and sat there, limp as a drunk, while they watched from the front window. Apparently his eyes were glassy and they were worried he would have a fit. Eventually he got up and walked to your car. When he drove off he didn't look back. Has he anywhere else to go?'

'No.'

'There's more. The police.'

'They know?'

'They were leaving when I arrived. A neighbour had rung them, I suppose. It was Lightfoot; he's all right but he was saying that Ratcliffe was cracking down on everyone at the moment.'

'What harm was done, Celia – a vase, two buttons? There was no need for the police.'

'Breach of the peace? Theft? Nothing broken but the law.'

'I always knew the Thucs would be a dead end. If you were Croft, how would you have reacted?'

She looked at me reprovingly, knowing I could not seriously expect her to answer such a question. 'Will you let me see the girl?' she asked.

'She has nothing to do with this.'

'Don't be exasperating. She has *everything* to do with it.'

'You know what I mean. She's the still eye of this little storm.'

Celia turned a quizzical eye on me. 'That's a rather grand, melodramatic way of putting it, Maurice. What makes you think storm centres have nothing to do with what revolves around them?'

Quite suddenly, I was angry. 'I warn you, Celia, don't make use of Kim. Otherwise you and I will become enemies. I mean it.'

She clicked her tongue. 'Please, spare me the attitudinising. I should be offended – when have I ever used you, or what you stood for, or what you believed in? You should learn to recognise your friends, Maurice, otherwise you'll always be half-blind. Now, may I talk to Miss Croft, please?'

Abashed, but still reluctant, I led the way to the cottage and made the introductions. The first thing Kim did was ask about Croft. Celia told her that she had talked to the Thucs; that he had been there; she did not mention any trouble. Kim looked directly at me. 'What happened?' she asked.

'They couldn't help. I'm sorry, Kim.'

She nodded, suddenly preoccupied, and brought her hand up to her mouth. We watched as she put a knuckle between her teeth.

Celia began to ask one or two gentle questions, none of them too leading. I stood beside Kim like a guardian, ready to protest if I thought that the interview was becoming too unfair or distressing. Another car drew up outside. I walked quickly to the window, thinking that Croft had returned, but he had not.

There were two policemen. One of them, Lightfoot, I had met before; he was the one Ratcliffe had sent into the water to recover the body of the Edmondson girl. Later he had told me how the incident had upset him, and how the girl had reminded him of his own sister. Ratcliffe had only been cursorily sympathetic, and for some time appeared to think that the girl need not have drowned. At the inquest he had merely spoken of police procedure and safety advice, and had not even seemed aware of the parents sitting nearby.

The two policemen had a relaxed, friendly manner. I was on my guard immediately, for I knew from my own experience how this could fool people into sharing confidences. I told them the essentials of what I knew, but omitted the tale of the clairvoyant and Croft's speculations on how close the Thucs could be to Kim. I also told them that I had given him permission to use the car. I did not believe this to be a full lie.

Kim was asked several questions as well. Each of them she handled with aplomb, making me think that it was not the first time she had been asked awkward questions. She also said that she was sure there had been some mistake, that Croft (she called him *Dad*) was a calm, unruffled character, and had been like that for as long as she had known him.

'I'm sure you're right, miss,' Lightfoot said. He was talking with such a broad accent I wondered if Kim would have difficulty understanding him. 'But for whatever reason, there seems to have been some kind of disagreement with your, err, distant cousins. We can't have that sort of thing going on, you know. It *is* against the law.'

'And with all due respect, miss,' his companion went on, picking up the thread; 'if he fought in Vietnam he must have learned quite a few nasty tricks. If he lost his temper, he could be really dangerous.'

'Dad never fought in Vietnam,' Kim said.

Perhaps the policemen did not notice our reaction, for Celia and I exchanged startled glances. Evidently Kim's remark made no real difference to their understanding of the case. 'Be that as it may, miss,' Lightfoot continued; 'for all I know of that war it was a bad affair all round. Violence may be a way of life out there, but it's not the kind of thing we like to see on our patch.' He turned to me. 'When do you expect him, reverend?'

'I don't know.'

'Your guess is as good as ours, sergeant,' Celia said.

The policemen looked at each other and Lightfoot rather ostentatiously consulted his watch. 'We have better things to do than sit round all day,' he explained. 'Everyone has been told to look out for Mr Croft anyway.'

'That's something of an over-reaction isn't it, sergeant?' I asked.

'I would have thought you'd have been pleased to get your car back, sir,' Lightfoot answered drily. 'If he turns up, you will tell him we want to see him, won't you?'

'Of course.'

He turned to Celia. 'Your usual discretion, I'm sure.' Celia nodded and smiled in acknowledgement. 'You'll phone?' he asked me.

'I promise.'

They said their goodbyes and sat in the car for a couple of minutes while one spoke on the radio, then they drove off.

I was still astonished at what Kim had told us. 'I thought Luciano was a soldier,' I said. 'He was bound to have been in battle. Everyone was, weren't they?'

'Didn't he tell you?' Celia asked me.

I shook my head.

'He doesn't hide it,' Kim said. 'You can't have asked him.'

'What did he do?' Celia asked.

She shrugged. 'The nearest he ever got to battle was talking to those who had fought them. Although, of course, there were the bombs, and towards the end the mortars and the gunfire. He sat at a desk all the time he was out there. Why would you think he was a soldier?'

I raised my hands helplessly. 'It was the obvious conclusion to draw.'

'Was it? Does he act like a soldier?'

We could not answer that.

'He sat at a desk in the Embassy and processed forms. Just like he did when we lived in London.'

'He was a diplomat,' Celia said crisply. 'Well, well, well.'

'Sure he was a diplomat. He was one of the people you had to see if you wanted out of the country. He had a photo of the President on his desk and a big Stars and Stripes on the wall behind him. It was his job to select the ones who could go. That was why he was there at the end – he had the power to issue passes. He had power over lots of people.'

My vision blurred. 'The people round the helicopter – would they have been given permits?'

'Maybe. I don't know if they managed to lift everyone off who had them. I think they did, and a few more as well.'

'Luciano said that, towards the end, there were people scaling the walls. They were the ones he'd refused?'

'There were more than him who issued them; you must ask him about that. I'm really not sure what happened.'

Already I was imagining them crowding the lift-off area, crazed with fear and betrayal. And I was wondering if Croft himself had given a pass to the woman and her baby, or if he had refused them one. Perhaps his guilt was more immediate and more personal than either I had suspected or he had admitted.

'Maurice?'

It was Celia's voice, but to my ears it was strangely distorted, as if she spoke under water.

Confused, I turned to her and saw all the colours of the room blur. She spoke my name again. I could hear urgency and concern in her voice, but it sounded as if it had travelled from a long way away.

A dizzying, unfocussed vision swept over me. I was gasping for breath in air that was being chopped and compressed, as if by the scything of massive blades. The air broke and fell, as if it rode breakers and could plunge and lift. I had my hands grasping something which seemed distant, and I could feel that they were cold and that fronds moved around my wrists like seaweed. At my back the darkness was cavernous. Quite suddenly I pulled upwards and Kim's face came bursting out of a swell of mottled greyness and loomed up towards me. She had the face she had now, and her eyes were closed and her mouth gasped like an infant denying itself air.

A voice spoke close to my ear. 'Maurice.'

The vision drained away. I was sprawled on the ground, and, not recognising the ceiling of my own cottage, for a few moments I did not know where I was.

Celia appeared, two-dimensional and unreal. I closed my eyes as tightly as I could, thinking perhaps that I would catch the remnants of the vision – the noise of helicopters, perhaps. But all I could hear was a distant rhythmic sound, like that of the sea.

'Did you faint?' Celia asked me.

I could not answer because I did not know.

Between them Celia and Kim lifted me to my feet and then helped me to the couch. For a while the room buckled and swayed around me and I had to sit with my eyes closed and my hands resting on the couch arm so that I could tell exactly where I was.

'Should I call a doctor?' Celia asked.

'No,' I said, for the moment unable to shake my head. 'It's passing off. In five minutes I'll be fine.'

But I still did not know if my imagination had overwhelmed me or if I had been granted insight.

6

THAT AFTERNOON KIM AND I SAT ON THE BENCH
in front of the cottage, looking across the reserve
with the sun full on our faces. I had answered a
phone call from Celia, who was merely checking
that I was all right, but, other than that, all was
quiet. Kim was silent for some time. When I asked if
she was certain that Croft would return, she replied
that she was certain that he would. 'You shouldn't
think you've been conned,' she said. 'Lucky's kind of
driven, that's all. Different rules apply to him. Often
I have to act as go-between for him and the rest of
the world. Sometimes it doesn't work out.'

'Most of us don't know what being driven
means, Kim. It's our ambition to lead ordinary, unpre-
dictable lives. Only in dreams are we men of great
deeds, and few dare realise them. Look at me. I've
achieved nothing.' I sat for more than a minute,
thinking back over the vivid sensations that had swept
through me just a few hours before. I had begun to
wonder if they were something to do with death. 'I'll
end my life here, at the very edge of England, and

all that will be left of me are a few memories which will soon wither, a series of mentions in the files of the local press, my name in the parish registers. That will be it.'

'You have a family. Your family will remember you, and carry on your name.'

'No. I have a daughter I haven't seen for years, and who I'll not see again; Grandchildren to whom I'm just a dim memory mixed up with cold and rain, and who I wouldn't even recognise.' I was surprised at my own candour, and remembered how a Catholic priest had once told me that the best confessions were always made to strangers. 'I thought I could write a book about religion that was honest, direct, and free of cant and deceit. I got no further than a few scribbled notes. After that I narrowed my aims, and believed I could construct a complete taxonomy of this little patch of earth. Something that would be exhaustively detailed, encyclopaedic. I thought that whole ecosystems, whole pyramids of life could be inferred by such minute specifics. Instead, I do the occasional article for the local press on the breeding habits of gulls, or shells washed up on the beach, or the number of times we are raided by a fox.'

'You're unhappy?'

'Resigned, perhaps. I'm not quite sure what happiness is, although my daughter believes she has found it. I wonder about cutting myself free from everyone, Kim, but I recognise that would be a kind of romanticisation of my own failure. For most of my working life I've tried to make God, Christ, more immediate and more secular. I tried to make them *appropriate* in this kind of world. Now there's a certain appeal to the idea of dying like a hermit. A hundred years after I've gone, the tracks of beetles across sand dunes will still look exactly the same. Gulls will still rear their young as they have done for thousands and thousands of generations. That's the real holiness of life – its diversity, its beauty and intricacy. That's the only real immortality.'

'You couldn't cut yourself off from everyone. What would Celia do?'

'Celia?'

'Isn't that her name?'

'Yes, that's what she's called. But she has nothing to do with me. We're friendly, that's all. We could live without each other very easily.'

Kim said nothing.

'The truth is, I'm suspicious of her at times.' I watched the sun slide imperceptibly down the sky. Shadows were already pointing towards us. 'I'm being a bore,' I said some time later. 'Why, you're forty years younger than me, more, and yet you've been to places and seen things that I'll never see. You even came from a part of the world where wars were fought over politics and religion, and there was I, safe in my little corner, preaching that religions are localised, with functions specific to the society from which they spring, and that you cannot change a man's religion without changing his life. Most of my friends from college moved away from where they had been born, but I was always more interested in what lay just in front of us. If you stare at the horizon, you miss what lies at your feet.'

'Your daughter did that?'

'After her divorce she went to India with the children. I thought it was a harebrained, dangerous thing to do. Years later, I look back and see that it may have had something to do with me.' I thought of how, all those years ago, I had believed that Jessica would grow up to love me more than I had ever been able to love my own parents. Later she was to accuse me of selfishness, of demanding more than I was able to give, of repressive tolerance. The search for God, I thought, is often the search for the father.

'She still writes you. All those letters – I saw them in the rack there.'

'Jessica is one of those people who used to be tongue-tied when she was with others, but always poured out her heart and her fantasies in a diary. I'm sure she must find it all very therapeutic.'

'And your grandchildren?'

Indoctrinated, I thought; their heads crammed with the vague, the insubstantial, a mush that smothers the intelligence. 'I mean what I say. I'll never see them again.'

I put my fingers to my brow. It was damp with sweat.

'Perhaps she is more free,' Kim said at last.

'Free? I gave her a liberal upbringing, and this is how she repays me.'

'Does that mean that you did not raise her as a Christian?'

'Of course I did. But I told her about Buddha and Shiva and Zoroaster as well. It seemed, at the time, that that was the wisest, kindest thing to do. I thought she would grow to see that orthodox Christian beliefs, at least in the way in which many see them, are juvenile and misleading. Instead, she turned to absurd mystification, to folly. Of all people, she should have known better. I couldn't blame my parishioners when they rejected what I had to say, but I expected more from Jessica.'

'I think, Maurice, that you have turned your back on many people.'

'It was the congregation that turned its back on me. There were complaints to my bishop – anonymous notes saying I had evil, unChristian views. Everything came to a head when one of my people lost their little girl in an accident. It was one of those terrible, senseless events that happen all the time. The family were distraught, and asked me how God could allow such a thing – they had always gone to church, always tried to be good, never fought or stole or behaved like bad citizens. Their simplicity was astounding. They wanted me to say that God worked in mysterious ways, that their little girl would be in heaven that night, sitting among the angels. I couldn't lie to them any more. I told them the truth; I told them what I believed. Of course it made everything far worse.'

'You brought the crisis on yourself. Why couldn't you lie? Lucky says he would lie to get his way. He says the end justifies the means.'

I was so engrossed in self-pity that I did not fully register what she had said. Instead, I continued with my own tale. 'That Sunday I got up in the pulpit and made a public confession. I told them that the essence of Christianity had been lost within a smokescreen of folklore, myth, supernatural accretion. I told them that a series of mandarin councils had ossified the spirit of the faith. I said that a lot of things they believed were unnecessary and false – the virgin birth, the miracles, resurrection, the promise of eternal life. That there was a Christian morality by which we should live our lives, but that it was secular, difficult, concerned purely with this world. That there was no such thing as divine intervention, no teleological pattern to life. That when we died there was oblivion, nothing else, and that the best that could be said was that we returned to a kind of background energy that was gradually seeping away as the universe ran down.

I delivered myself into their hands. After that, I couldn't stay.'

'I was brought up without a religion.'

'I see no harm in that.'

'My passport says that I am a Buddhist. Lucky and his wife believed that I should be able to return to whatever religion I was to begin with. Buddhism seemed the most appropriate. But I may have been baptised – who knows?'

'Does it worry you?'

'No, because I do not want to return to what I was. The past is dead.'

I looked closely at her. She had her eyes closed against the sunshine; I could see the pupils tremble beneath the lid. 'I do not know why I was given away,' she went on; 'but there must have been a reason. It cannot have just been opportunity. Not everything is the random workings of chance. Perhaps my mother knew someone in the helicopter, or had a lover in the marines, or worked for the Americans. Lucky just happened to be the nearest to her. There are worse possibilities. My father may have worked for the death squads, he may have been a criminal supported by the Embassy, my mother may have been a prostitute. Many of those who came out were murderers and corrupt officials. I no longer wish to think about it, but I have to think about it all the time.'

'Do you wish it would end, Kim?'

'Do I show that?'

'It's a suspicion, not an observation.'

'I feel I'm standing on the edge of something I don't recognise, and that Lucky is behind me, forcing me to leap into the dark. I don't want that at all. I want to live an ordinary life, to settle down. Does that seem an extraordinary thing for someone my age to say? I mean it. I want to be able to make friends, to say to someone – anyone – that I'll meet them in a week's time at a certain place and know that I'll be there. I want to go to college, graduate, get a good job. I can't have any of that until we reach some kind of conclusion. I have lived for too long not knowing where the next plane or train or boat would take us, and when.'

'Many would be jealous of you.'

'Only the foolish. Tell me, Maurice, do you think I'm mature beyond my years? Do I act my age?'

'Sometimes. Not often.'

'I act younger than my years sometimes, but usually I have to act older. I don't want to do that. I don't want to know what the Himalayas look like from a plane, or the Coral Sea, or the Northern Territories. I want to go out with girlfriends, ring boys up on the phone, spend money on stuff that's not important. I want to have fun, be flippant, take up my life where I had to leave it the day we took the ashes back to the States. Soon it will be too late to do that.'

'If you did that, surely you'd always wonder about your parents, about who you were?'

'I know who I am. I'm Kim Croft, of Vietnamese parentage, a naturalised American. I belong among Americans, not among Asians. I can't go back, just like you couldn't go back and undo all that has already been done. It's gone, vanished, dead. My parents would be strangers to me. They'd speak a different language, one I don't know any more. Eat different food. Live a different life. It's pointless to pretend otherwise.'

'Have you told Luciano this?'

'He'll not listen. He no longer thinks sensibly about what we are doing. He sees us more like chesspieces on a board.'

'He really believes that sort of stuff?'

'Of course. That's the only way in which he can make sense of what has happened to us.'

I shook my head. 'He's wrong. We all make our own choices, for good or ill. We shouldn't appeal to God or fate or some mystical causal principle for the reason for our actions. We carry the responsibility – you, me, Luciano, the Thucs, all of us.'

'Responsibility? And whose responsibility is it to keep me here?'

She was staring ahead at the dunes, her eyes half-closed. I did not know what to say.

'In Sydney there was a boy who wanted me to stay. He told me that he cared a lot for me, and talked of escaping with me to a sanctuary in the outback, where we would live like castaways. It was just a dream.'

'Luciano took you away.'

'He wasn't for me. He was from Saigon too, you see. But I let Lucky take the decision, just as he takes all the decisions. Whatever he tells me to do, I go along with.' Then she turned to me. Sun caught the strands of her black hair and made it gleam. 'What would he do if he came back here and found me gone?'

'You can't desert him. His whole life is built on you.'

'Built on a solution to me, you mean. Would you hide me, Maurice? Cover for me? Would I be worth lying for?'

'You know I can't do that.'

She had been sharp and intense, but now it appeared that the energy had suddenly left her. 'No,' she said quietly; 'of course you can't.'

We sat and watched the sun descend towards the sea.

The phone rang twice that evening; the police checked that we had heard nothing further, and Celia called again to see if I was still all right. Of Croft there was no sign.

I told Kim I would leave the back door open, just in case. After she had gone to bed, however, I felt I should bolt it; only my promise prevented me from doing so.

For an hour I lay awake with the curtains open, and only gradually did I fall asleep. As on the previous night, I woke up in the early hours. A wind was eddying round the house, and from far away came the noise of breakers crashing on the shore. After a few minutes came a shrill, unidentifiable cry; from its clarity and sharp termination I guessed it was an animal killed by a predator. I tried to concentrate my senses so that they were focussed inside the house. Nothing seemed amiss.

I got out of bed and walked to the living-room. The curtains were open, although I could remember having closed them. On the couch was a regular, flattened shape. 'Luciano?' I asked, but even as I spoke I remembered that I had left a blanket folded across the seat in case he returned.

I went to the back door and slid the bolt home. Then I stood at the door to the spare room, wondering whether to call and ask Kim if she was all right or push the door so that I could peer inside. I waited too long for either decision, and soon felt myself to be a foolish, overcautious old man, worrying ridiculously about someone who was much better travelled than I would ever be. I went back to my own bed and within a few seconds had fallen asleep. I heard the early-morning train travel along the line, but it did not really disturb me.

It was later than usual when I woke, aware that I had overslept but with no real sense of what the time was. Only when I peered at the clock did I realise that it was half-past eight, and that someone was knocking at the front door.

I answered in my pyjamas, hoping that Kim would not be sitting in the living-room to see me like that. I was sure I would look frail, unattractive and faintly despicable. Everything was just as it had been left – the blankets were squared on the sofa, the door to Kim's room was closed, and the curtains were open onto a calm and sunny day.

I slid the bolt and opened the door, certain that Luciano Croft would be standing there, weary and contrite. It was Celia.

'You look surprised,' she said with an air of mild rebuke.

'Did you say you would call? I'd forgotten.'

'Maurice, if I couldn't see for myself that you were all right you know I'd just worry about you. You weren't answering your phone, anyway.'

'I didn't hear it. I suppose I must have been really tired after yesterday. So you drove all this way? There was no need.'

I went back to my bedroom to get changed, and was careful to close the door behind me. When I came out Celia was making tea. 'How many is this for?' she asked.

'Three, if Kim's awake. No, he didn't turn up; no, he didn't ring.'

'I see.'

'Aren't you due at your office?'

'I don't work regular hours. Should just the two of us drink this?'

We sat on the couch and drank the tea Celia had made. She sat closer to me than usual. 'You'll have to look after yourself, Maurice. You're isolated here. I keep hearing lots of horror stories of people who have had strokes and lain for days unable to reach a phone.'

'A stroke? I haven't had a stroke.'

'Let's call it a temporary interruption of blood supply to the brain, then.'

'I fainted. It had been a strenuous day.'

'That doesn't invalidate what I say. I have work to do; I can't be your guardian angel all of the time.'

I was perplexed. Celia was taking more interest in my welfare than I would have thought. I had believed her sole concern was for a story out of Croft or Kim.

'You lost all your colour,' she went on, 'the girl and I were quite worried.'

'Celia, I'm content here. I'm not leaving.'

'It's up to you, but you should think it through more logically. When all this is sorted out, when the

Crofts have gone, you'll have more time to think. You've been here a few years now, and none of us are getting any younger. They say that when a summer is hot, the next winter will be more harsh.'

'They say it the other way round. And there's nothing to think about, because I'm staying.'

She reached out and put her finger to my lips to stop me from continuing. It was the first time Celia had touched me, apart from a handshake. The touch of her finger gave me an unexpected and unsettling jolt. Not wishing to look at her, I looked away to the far wall.

'Promise me,' she said. I was looking at the phone.

I did not need to say anything. She turned on the couch, following my gaze. A coil of wire lay beneath the small table on which the phone stood.

Celia walked across to it and lifted the cable, which had been severed as if by a knife. It looped uselessly across her hand. She turned, about to ask me a question, but then strode quickly to Kim's room and opened the door without knocking. I followed her as quickly as I could.

There was no one there.

The bed had been slept in, and the sheets were crumpled and rolled halfway down as if they had been pushed back roughly. Her clothes had gone, her radio, and her bag. There was no trace of her at all except for a distant, pleasant smell of perfume which underlined her absence. She had gone.

I was shocked and betrayed. I had not believed she would desert me like this, fleeing during the night without even a parting word for all the kindness and consideration I had shown.

'You didn't expect this,' Celia said.

'Of course not.'

'She gave no indication?'

'No. She talked about what she would like to do. She was daydreaming, I suppose.'

'Croft, do you think? Would he have come back for her?'

'I don't know. She could have caught the early train. It stops just a mile up the line.'

The more I thought about it, the more certain I was that Kim had met up with Croft. I could not understand their alliance. I had thought it to be something made in accordance with the circumstances in which they found themselves; he alternately desperate and hopeful, she resentful yet accepting, each of them willing to leave the other to their own devices for a certain length of time but no more. What would they do now, I wondered, having found that the Thucs were a false lead, a coincidence, nothing more? I thought of the two of them meeting, like spies, at a prearranged place and time, possibly the very railway platform I had first met them on. I imagined them laughing, and comparing how they had each left me in exactly the same way. On the train south they would agree that I was a foolish old man, unworldly and provincial. I imagined them returning again to that fragile network of contacts, speculation and chance which had borne them across much of the world and would continue to bear them in their endless quest. I would never be able to forget either of them.

Celia and I stood at the door like two soldiers wearied after a battle. 'That's it, then,' I said simply. There was nothing else I could say.

'There are a few details still. Your car, for instance.'

'It'll turn up, abandoned. I don't know why the phone was cut. It was so unnecessary.'

'She thought you would warn the police, that's why. She was scared, or he was, that you would turn him in. Let's face it, Maurice, those two have been pretty professional in the way they have treated us. They've worked like confidence men.' As she spoke, her voice faltered and strength seemed to ebb from it.

'What's the matter?' I asked.

She was staring at me, but her expression was strange. 'I drove past the refuse bin by the reserve entrance,' she said. 'Do you ever use it?'

'Sometimes. I pick up cartons that get left on the dunes, things like that.'

'Found anything recently?'

I shook my head. I could not follow this sudden shift in our discussion.

Celia walked back outside, got in her car, and reversed quickly down the road. I hurried along after her, disturbed by her strange behaviour.

She was standing next to the fence when I caught up with her, looking down onto the baked earth. There was a small, white leather shoe lying there. I felt suddenly weak.

'I noticed it when I drove past,' Celia said, her voice buckling with anticipation; 'but I thought nothing of it. Is it hers?'

'I don't know. She wore shoes just like it, though.'

I bent down, but Celia touched my arm to stop me. 'Better not,' she said.

'Why?'

'Fingerprints, I suppose. You know what the police are like.'

'Why should they wish to take fingerprints from this?' I asked, but already my mind was filling with darkness.

Celia reached into her car and brought out a cheap plastic pen. With its tip she lifted the spring-top to the refuse bin, and peered inside the black plastic liner. 'And these?' she asked.

I looked inside, my heart thumping furiously. Within the bin was a knotted jumble of clothes. Beneath them the corner of a travel bag could be seen. Flies rose in the air around us.

I stepped back and closed my eyes. The world had

set itself at a new, frightening angle, and when I grasped a fence post as support it felt slack and useless.

Celia took hold of my arm. 'Do you want to lean on me?'

I shook my head but still felt faint.

'They're Kim's, aren't they?' she asked.

I nodded. I could not speak.

7

THE ROOM WAS SMALL, NO BIGGER THAN A CELL, with bare walls and a tiny high window of clouded glass. Lightfoot ushered me in, then motioned me to sit down to one side of a long wooden table. I did so, and leaned back against the wall. He addressed me as if I were an accident victim, and said that he would bring me a cup of tea. I shook my head but he insisted, in a slightly chiding voice, that it would be best for me – he was making Celia one as well.

When he had gone I looked round the room. A strip light burned in the ceiling, but the switch was outside in the corridor. A battered metal ashtray had been left on one side of the table. There was a scratch on the inside of the door and one or two triangular chips in the wall that showed the grain of the plaster beneath the paint. The walls and door were so thick that I could hear very little of what went on outside, although every now and then there was the noise of people passing down the corridor. I felt strangely isolated, on unfamiliar ground. When I had been brought in it was by the front entrance. All the uniformed officers, except Lightfoot, had behaved as if I was not there.

A few minutes later Lightfoot came back with a large mug of tea which he put down in front of me. 'There you are, sir,' he said, 'Inspector Ratcliffe will be along in a few minutes.'

'Will you be staying?'

'Not me, sir. The Inspector wants an informal chat, friend to friend like, if it's all right with you. Well, we all know each other of old, don't we? There are times when that's an advantage.'

I sipped the tea. It was very hot, and I almost burned my mouth. 'What about Mr Croft?' I asked.

'We're looking after him,' he said, cheerily neutral.

'He's in a cell?'

'You could say that, sir.' He put his hands in his pockets and looked thoughtful. 'I've got a feeling that this may turn out to be not very pleasant at all,' he said, with the air of a disappointed politician.

'I'm sure you're wrong,' I said, with more certainty than I felt. 'When do I get my car back?'

'That depends on when our lads have finished with it. There is nothing wrong with it, though – no dents, no scrapes, and the tank is almost full. He even left the keys in the ignition. Not like your usual theft.'

'I told you the other day, it wasn't a theft.'

'If you say so, sir. We still want to hang on to it for a while.'

'And Mr Croft? How long will you want to hang on to him?'

'Oh,' he said, drawing out the sound; 'that depends, now.'

'What are you holding him for? It can't be theft, because I would refute that. Breach of the peace, could it be?'

Lightfoot smiled at me but did not reply. I picked up the tea and blew across its surface, watching the tiny ripples my breath made. Suddenly I remembered my own father doing just such an action, and I recalled how, when I was older, I had been repelled by his habit because I considered it uncouth. I put the mug down so sharply that liquid slopped onto the table. 'He *is* under arrest, then?'

Lightfoot nodded, then leaned forward confidentially. 'Between you and me, when I walked up to him on the platform he fainted clean away. I had to hold his feet up until he came round. It caused quite a stir among the other people waiting for the train, I can tell you. He was still groggy when it pulled out.'

'The Euston train?'

He nodded again.

'It sounds like the reaction of an innocent man, to me.'

'You never can tell about things like that, reverend. I wouldn't be so quick jumping to such a conclusion. When we brought him in we took away his belt, his watches, his wallet, and handed him the leaflets – all the usual practice, you understand – and we made him leave his shoes outside the cell door. That's enough to make most people very unhappy, very vulnerable. But a few minutes later I had a look through the judas when he wasn't looking. Our man was dancing. Well, not *dancing* exactly, but he was strutting up and down like a drum majorette, walking backwards and forwards as if he was prancing. Quite light on his feet, he was.'

'What does he say about it?'

It was the wrong question to ask. Lightfoot immediately retreated from his confidential posture. 'I'm sure I wouldn't know that,' he replied, rather stiffly. Then, as if he detected sounds I could not hear, he opened the door slightly and peered down the corridor. 'I'll have to go now, sir,' he said. 'But the Inspector will be with you shortly.'

After he had left I sat and drank my tea. I tried to picture Croft arrested at the railway station, Croft pacing his cell, but the images obstinately refused to come alive. His arrest, though, was assuming an importance greater than that of a man who had merely scuffled, perhaps fought, with someone else. His potential crime, the one I feared most of all, had never been mentioned and scarcely been hinted at. Nevertheless, it hung in the air, invisible, and it seemed that by talking about him I would begin the process of delineating its outline.

Ratcliffe came in about ten minutes later. 'Maurice,' he said, and shook my hand. This time his grip lingered, as if a moment's extra contact would somehow place me in his debt or draw from me some piece of information which would be otherwise inaccessible. 'Well, well,' he said, sitting down and exhaling as if he was just settling into a favourite armchair; 'when was it we last met? Earlier this year?'

'All this was just starting.'

'Really?' Beneath the feigned relaxation he was prickly with alertness. 'You'll have to tell me about that.' His accent had been thickened, possibly deliberately, since I last talked to him. It made him sound more homely and less bright.

'Harry, what are you accusing him of?'

He looked vague, like someone about to invent a reply. 'I don't know; we'll have to see what comes out of all this. I have my suspicions, though.'

'I wasn't born yesterday,' I complained, and he raised a quizzical eyebrow. 'The girl could be anywhere.'

'That's right. You think I want to talk to you about the girl?'

'I think you're playing with me. You're convinced

that harm has come to her. You have no real evidence.'

Ratcliffe pulled the ashtray towards him. The metal squeaked on the wood. Then he lit a cigarette and made a dismissive gesture with the hand that held it. 'Instinct alone would tell me something was wrong, but the evidence supports a theory that's, well, let me say pessimistic. There are the clothes you mentioned. Tossed in, as if thrown from the back of a car. There's your car, abandoned outside the main station. And there's Luciano Croft, apprehended just a couple of minutes before he gets on the London train. The girl is nowhere to be seen; she's vanished from the face of the earth. Maurice, you must admit that the picture looks very black.'

'I don't know if I could agree with that. They're an extraordinary couple and they have ways of doing things that seem alien and strange to us. Perhaps Kim's in London now. Perhaps she's buying new clothes as we speak.'

'Perhaps. You told Lightfoot that your car wasn't stolen. Did you mean that?'

'I'm not in the habit of lying.' As I spoke I could feel a blush come to my cheeks, as if that very statement was an untruth and I had betrayed myself.

'You didn't know where or when he was going to leave it? There was no agreement, no understanding on that?'

'No.'

'I see. You will tell me everything, won't you? It's necessary.'

I knew he was staring hard at me and I felt myself redden further as I pretended to examine my fingers and flex them on the table. 'What's Croft telling you?' I asked after a few seconds, feeling the blood subside.

'Nothing. I mean that literally. He sits and says nothing at all.'

'He keeps completely silent, you mean?'

'That's right. Oh, don't worry, he'll talk all right. It's just a matter of time and circumstance.'

'Does he have to? He's an American citizen.'

'His rights are being honoured. American or not, he's still subject to British law.'

'He's a diplomat. He has immunity.'

'Celia Price told me that. But he didn't claim immunity, and he didn't even ask for a lawyer. We checked with the Embassy. He hasn't been in the diplomatic service for several years.' After a short pause he added, 'So he's fair game, Maurice. I'd appreciate your help.'

'I don't even know what he's supposed to have done, and yet you ask me to help you.'

'We each have our own suspicions, though, don't we? Isn't it a coincidence that, when we met outside the courts, this whole sequence of events had started to unfold? According to you, that is. What were you doing there, Maurice – was that when you first mentioned him to the Thucs?'

I nodded wearily. 'I've already gone through this.'

'With Lightfoot – yes, I know. But I want to hear it all from your own lips. And besides, everything has changed since you talked to Lightfoot.'

'All right. Yes, that was the day I'd tried to get help from the Thucs. You know all about them, I suppose.'

'Strange name, isn't it? Sounds like a cheese biscuit. I'm sorry, Maurice – I forgot you were a sensitive soul over such matters, and maybe I'm not as cosmopolitan as I should be. Go on.'

I wanted to tell him that I would not be joshed into an artificially easy relationship just by a few jokily offensive phrases. I let it pass, however, and merely summarised what had happened between them and me. As I spoke I began to realise that I had been peripheral to the entire enterprise, and that my part in it had been defined by the actions of others. I thought of a hand, placed on a cave wall and drawn round with charcoal, then taken away; if I wanted to imagine a representation of my own self, I would have to think of a picture of a hand on a wall.

Towards the end of my narrative I faltered once or twice, but Ratcliffe never interrupted. Several times he appeared to have lost interest; instead he studied the blank ceiling, or the smoke curling from his dying cigarette, or else he rotated the ring round his finger. I guessed that these actions were mere camouflage, and that from behind their screen he would be observing with me a sharply analytic eye.

When I had finished he waited a while and then asked 'Is that all?' like a man disappointed by an inferior variety act.

I spread my hands to indicate completeness.

He looked at the ring, pursed his lips, and waited for several seconds before putting his next question. 'Are you sure there's nothing else?'

'I don't think so.'

'You know the kind of question I'm supposed to ask you, Maurice. I'm supposed to ask you do you remember anything strange or unusual or unexpected. I have to put that to you.'

'Their whole situation was like that.'

'Something that, in retrospect, gave the game away?'

'No.'

He sighed deeply. 'It seems plain that he's killed her, Maurice. I don't know why. All I can do, so far, is speculate.'

I could feel a chill rise through me, like the fear of water in a man who cannot swim.

'*You* don't know, do you?'

'I have no idea. If he did.'

'What would you say were your feelings towards them?'

I tried to find words that would adequately summarise how I felt about the Crofts, but before I could even start Ratcliffe spoke again.

'You pitied them,' he said, with a finality that left no room for the remark to be a suggestion.

'No. No, it wasn't as simple as that.'

'Envied them?'

I felt myself lick my lips nervously. 'Partly. But my feelings don't have anything to do with why we're here.'

He extended one hand and seesawed it to indicate that perhaps this was true, perhaps not.

'Do they?' I asked.

'Perhaps you were a kind of catalyst. Without knowing it.'

'I was someone they stayed with, that's all. Maybe they took advantage of me, as well.'

'Was that difficult to come to terms with – being taken advantage of, I mean? Do you find it a blow to your pride, an insult to your morality?'

'It's probably true that Luciano Croft had earned the right not to conform to normal patterns of behaviour. I understand that side of him.'

As soon as I had said it, I realised what Ratcliffe could say next. Although I waited, he said nothing, but looked at me, a slight smile on his face, as if he anticipated my every move. 'Well?' he asked at last.

Stubbornly, I kept my silence.

'You really should make sure that such comments aren't followed up by your questioner, Maurice. Do you wish to say more, or do I have to ask the obvious?'

'All right – no, I'm *not* saying that he therefore had a moral right to injure people. Or to kill them. That would be extending charity too far.'

'As well as being evil and stupid. I have a professional interest in motivation, of course. I like to see it running in a line between points, joining together events that would otherwise remain isolated. A bit like lines on a map, you might say.'

'And Croft? What about your professional interest in him?'

'I have to confess, Maurice, that I'm still in the dark about why your friend turned to murder, but I've no doubt at all that he did. So thank you for your assistance.'

'Is that it?'

'Celia Price is next door. Join her if you want.'

I started to rise, but he stopped me.

'In a few minutes,' he added.

I sat down again. I had thought the interview to be at an end, for there seemed little else I could tell Ratcliffe.

He stared at his ornate ring for a while, then began to speak again, picking his words carefully. 'I've been in this business a long time now. Long enough to look forward to retirement, anyway. I've learned that there are times when a man doesn't know what's going on around him, times when he doesn't really see what's happening. You agree?'

'Perhaps. Why?'

'Even the most ordinary, everyday words, phrases can be used to hide things. You'd be surprised at how people describe evil or nastiness. They use the most inoffensive descriptions.'

I could not see his point. 'Yes?'

'Maurice, you're a man who has lived on his own for – what, several years now?'

'Quite a few.'

'And when you were a vicar you didn't have a good reputation. I'm sorry, but you know that's true. It was said you didn't know what the needs of your congregation were. They thought you aloof, incapable of handling their welfare.'

'That was when the Edmondsons complained.'

'Not really. There were rumours years before that. The Edmondson case was, I suppose, the last straw.'

I was too astonished to be insulted. I had always believed that the rebellion against me had been spontaneous, and not the culmination of years of resentment

CHRISTOPHER BURNS

and mistrust. I had not realised the feeling against me was so deep-rooted.

'It could be that you're not the best at picking up or understanding what goes on in the real world. You see what I'm driving at? You were presented with two people who were well out of the ordinary, a bit exotic even. People from a violent, faraway place. These weren't the kind you or I would normally meet, these were people out of *history*. Is it any real surprise that you didn't get the drift of what was going to happen?'

I was silent.

'You say Croft had some sort of right not to behave like the rest of us.'

'I wish I hadn't used that word.'

He held up a hand as if to reject my objection. 'How did he use that right?'

'I know what you're going to say. Firstly, that he took my car – '

'Stole it. No matter how much you may deny it, effectively, that's what he did. And secondly, he starts to harass a family who as far as I know are completely innocent. A family you once said you would protect. You didn't even conceal their address from him.'

It was true. What would the Thucs think of me now, I wondered, now that I had harboured some-one who had disrupted their settled life, threatened them, even fought with one of them?

'And the last act of this rampage is the murder of a girl he had said *he* would protect. At least I assume that American adoption procedures contain a clause about protection. It seems likely, wouldn't you agree?'

'Probably.'

'They were a unique couple, all right. No wonder you were won over by them. They had a quest, after all – a mission, a sense of purpose. In the end, which way did that purpose turn? Into deception and violence. And murder. Not very glorious, is it?'

'You're distorting things.'

He looked at me ingenuously. 'Am I? How? Tell me where I'm going wrong, Maurice.'

'You're a policeman. It's your job to see the worst in people.'

'And what did you, a former man of the church, see in Luciano Croft? Not someone who was calculating, foxy, a survivor? You didn't see a murderer, did you? And you'd still prefer to think that the girl was still alive. That's obvious.'

'Wouldn't you?'

'Sooner or later each of us has to face probabilities and certainties rather than live a fantasy.'

'If he's so calculating, why has he no alibi? Why does he take refuge in silence?'

'Everyone has points where their whole life changes. A lot of them are planned; people like you would hold religious ceremonies round them

143

– marriages, births, deaths. Croft's changes must have been more dramatic. The last one took place in between Kim leaving your house and when he dumped her clothes in a bin.'

'I don't follow.'

'He's in shock. What would be going round your head if you were him? Remorse? Self-preservation?' Ratcliffe meshed his fingers and pushed his hands away from his body so the knuckles cracked under the strain. 'What led him here was this Australian information,' he said, pronouncing the last word as if it was a pure concept sullied by speculation and looseness.

'Yes.'

'Tell me that part again.'

I repeated the story of the clairvoyant, trying all the time to use the same phrases I had used at the first telling.

Afterwards Ratcliffe sat quietly, as if ruminating. 'Unbelievable, isn't it?' he said at last.

I did my best to remain impassive.

'Would you go flying across the world on the strength of the words of a witch woman? Celia told me this, as well. I find it difficult to believe that he arrived here because of what she said, and attacked the Thucs because of a story she had fabricated.'

'He had a chart with all the family connections on it. It will be with his belongings.'

'It was torn in four quarters and shoved in the bottom of the bin. The clothes were on top of it. Seems like he wanted to forget that as well.'

I could feel the strength drain from me. I wanted to curl up and ignore Ratcliffe, the police station, Luciano Croft.

'Men like us would have demanded harder evidence,' he went on. 'Perhaps he had it.'

I ignored him, but his stare was unmoving. Still I wanted to hide myself. I had begun to realise, with dreadful finality, that Kim was indeed dead, and that Croft had murdered her.

'He got to the end of his tether, I suppose,' I could hear Ratcliffe say. 'She held him until, at last, he disposed of her. He broke free.'

The fact of her death passed through me like a dark tide, and yet I could not visualise her lying dead. For that I needed a patch of ground, a room, part of a landscape in which to place her.

Dimly I became aware of Ratcliffe selecting another cigarette. He held it between his lips, lit it, and took his first inhalation in a systematic way, like someone trying to impress by ritual. 'Last night – how did he get in? Did she open the door for him?'

'We don't know he did,' I said stubbornly, like a man repeating a charm out of desperation rather than belief. 'We don't know what happened.'

'I think he would cut the wire, not her. Don't you? But how did he get in?'

'I left the door open.' It was a confession, and I felt the first rush of release before the dark began to close around me.

Ratcliffe looked directly at me, his expression unchanging.

'I suppose he just walked in,' I said, as defiantly as I could.

'Did she ask you to leave it open?'

'No.'

'So it was your idea.'

'Yes.'

'I see.'

I felt anguished with guilt. 'I bolted it during the night.'

'It was still bolted in the morning?'

I hesitated.

'I asked Celia. She says when she called you had to draw back the bolt.'

'She's right. Can't you see that I realise now it could all have been different?'

'Afterwards, people torment themselves by such thoughts. You're no different to others, and nothing I say will make anything any better for you. You haven't mentioned a struggle.'

'No.'

'You didn't hear one?'

146

'No.'

'A voice, a footstep?'

'The wind was blowing hard. It rose through the night.'

'There's not a breath of wind outside. Highly localised, was it?'

'You've lived on this coast for years; you know how conditions can change within a hundred yards.'

He nodded. 'She went willingly with him?'

'I don't know. How can I even speculate about that?'

'Perhaps she knew what would happen to her.'

'No, she wouldn't.'

'You're certain? Why?'

'She had everything to look forward to. She wanted to live a normal kind of life.'

'Away from him?'

'If necessary.'

'I understand. Exactly what *was* their relationship?'

'It's obvious.'

'Tell me.'

'She owed everything to him.'

'Including her life.'

'Yes. That's a terrible burden for anyone to carry.'

'Did she resent that? People sometimes do. Haven't you ever helped people who resented you, Maurice?'

'They showed each other extraordinary devotion. They're like father and daughter.'

He leaned forward, shuffling the weight over his elbows, which rested on the table. 'Do you think they were?'

I had sudden difficulty in breathing. 'They adopted Kim. He's her legal father, and his wife was her legal mother.'

'I mean genetically.'

I tried to scoff, but the sound came out absurdly, like a sneeze. 'The idea's laughable.'

'Is it? Isn't a man more likely to rescue his own child than that of a complete stranger?'

'Why? An act can be performed altruistically, selflessly, for the common good.'

'You don't get many selfless acts in police work.'

'Maybe you just don't recognise them.'

'You're telling me she's not his child?'

'Not in the sense that you mean.'

'A pity.' He tapped ash into the tray with careful timing. 'Everything would have much more understandable if she had been.'

I said nothing.

'He nearly got away with it; his luck failed him just a little too soon. You could be right about the girl. She could have gone quietly. Only an expert would have been able to take her without noise if she'd struggled.'

And I thought of a gull, lifted from its nest at night without a sound.

'She always did as she was told,' I said.

'It was straightforward, then.'

'Yes.'

'She didn't have an idea that he may do something violent? She didn't ask you for help – perhaps in a way that you didn't quite grasp at the time?'

I could feel his sly eyes weighing me up. I recalled, with unsettling detail, what Kim had said to me as we sat on the bench in front of the cottage. It had been less than a day ago.

'She asked for protection, didn't she? But you didn't recognise how serious it was.'

I put my hands to my face, not wanting to see him.

Ratcliffe whispered in my ear. I could smell his breath. 'We may need you later, Maurice. Join Celia Price if you wish, but don't leave the station. We need your knowledge of the reserve.'

Within a few minutes I had been shown into a room that was identical to the one I had just left. Celia stood as I entered. Her face showed strain and the pupils of her eyes had dilated. 'Are you all right?' she asked.

'Right as rain,' Lightfoot said, steering me towards the seat as if to a hospital bed; 'although I don't think you'll be leaving us just yet, will you sir?'

'No,' I said. Lightfoot nodded approval and left me alone with Celia, who sat beside me and took one of my hands between both of hers. I looked round, vaguely disorientated. Only the ceramic ashtray, discolorations of the paint, and a different pattern to the scratches on the door showed that I was in another room.

'What did Harry say?' Celia asked urgently.

'That Luciano had murdered Kim.'

'On the dunes?'

'I think so. Croft's said nothing, though.'

She was close to me. I could smell her perfume and see the grain of her skin. 'He told me he didn't think that would be a problem. He said that, in time, he'd produce the girl's clothes and lay them out on a table in front of Croft.'

'What?'

'It'll nudge him towards confession, Harry says.'

I looked askance at her. 'He thinks she's Lucky's daughter.'

There was a slight reaction, a tiny flinch, but not one of shock. He had suggested that to Celia as well, and she had not known if it had been put to me. She said nothing, but I could feel the grip tighten on my hand, as if she wished to hold on to me.

'He said it to you, as well.'

She hesitated for a few seconds. 'I wondered.'

'You *wondered*? What do you mean? You said nothing to me.'

Quite suddenly she appeared flustered, as if I had caught her out in some inefficiency. 'I didn't say anything to you – the chances of her being his seemed too remote. But she looked a little Western, don't you think? There seemed a trace of Mediterranean in her.'

I shook my head vigorously. 'You're imagining resemblances. I denied it.'

'He told me how he thought it could have happened. He worked out a whole theory just from information I gave him – a wartime liaison with a woman from another race, an unwanted child, the mother's last despairing attempt to save her. Harry said that if he had been willing to leave his mistress to her fate, then Croft must be a much colder man than either of us suspected.'

'Do you believe that?'

'How can I? He would have deserted the girl as well if he'd been like that. And he wouldn't have adopted her, or devoted his life to her.'

'And, in the end, when the Thucs slammed the door in his face?'

'Most other people would have cracked sooner, Maurice. Could anyone blame him for a fit of murderous despair?'

I looked at her and felt like a man trapped. 'What happened to me, Celia? I foresaw nothing like this. I harboured a murderer and his victim, and didn't even recognise it. He took my car, he attacked the

Thucs, and in the end I even left open the door so that he could come into my house in the night and take away the only innocent party in the whole sorry mess. She asked me for protection. On her last night alive, she asked me would I hide her, lie for her. But I was too busy feeling sorry for myself to see the danger she was in.'

'You mustn't torture yourself, Maurice. She may not have meant that. Girls of that age say unsettling and provocative things; it's part of growing up. You have no real evidence that would show she suspected Croft.'

'I thought of myself as a kind of wise hermit, parading my tiny kingdom by the sea, feeling morally superior, feeling that I was *right*. But that girl was a target. She was lined up as surely as if she was in a pair of shotgun sights.'

She took away one hand and put it on my shoulder. 'There's no need for this.'

I was tired and ill; I leaned towards her and she put a comforting arm round me. I wished I could forget everything; I wished I could expunge my entire life from just before the Edmondson girl drowned up until that moment; I wished that Celia would give me the comfort and security of a mother.

After my illness my mother had gone with me, holding my hand, for my first walk outside. She had wrapped me up with a woollen scarf round my neck and made sure my long socks were pulled up to just below my knees. Feeling uncertain and weak, I was scared that I might fall and held her hand. The sun was misty and liquid, and gleamed palely on the cobblestones; I remember, too, that its reflection bobbed and bounced as slow, langorous waves ran down the canal. I watched the waves passing beneath the footbridge with queasy elegance, and looked upstream. Until then I had not realised that a neighbour's child had gone missing, and that further up the banks men were trawling the water with grappling hooks.

My mother covered my eyes with her hand and hurried me away, our footfalls ringing in an eerie quiet, so I never saw the tiny body when it was recovered. But I recalled the event in vividly time-less detail when I watched Lightfoot wade into the river to reach the Edmondson girl. As he waded hip-deep through the water he seemed then to be entering my own destiny, to be acting out an event that had a meaning more deep and more cold than I could ever penetrate.

I looked up at Celia and heard my own voice as if from far away. 'The rock pool,' I said. 'He drowned her in the rock pool.'

8

NEVER BEFORE HAD THE RESERVE HAD SUCH VISITORS. We arrived in convoy, parking along the roadside beside the fence. Each car held two or more policemen, some in uniform, others in plain clothes. They congregated in small groups, their shadows hard-edged on the road, talking laconically to each other. A sense of expectation hung in the air.

Three men from the forensic team went into my cottage with their bags full of cameras and tweezers and plastic envelopes. I looked towards the viaduct and saw Celia's car pull up. Immediately, it was approached by two uniformed men who stood close to her as soon as she got out. I could hear her protestations carrying through the hot, still air. 'No press,' Ratcliffe shouted as I led the way onto the reserve.

Croft had arrived, wedged between two officers in the back of a car. When they got out I saw that he was handcuffed to one, and that the metal shone as brilliantly as silver. It was the first time I had seen him since he had lain on the couch in front of the dying fire and wished me goodnight. Now he kept his eyes down. He was silent, withdrawn, unshaven and white-faced. There was a puffiness beneath his eyes as if he had been weeping. He could have been a man being taken to his own death. The laces had been removed from his shoes and he walked with steps that were both clumsy and hesitant, like those of a comedian. One of his guards talked quietly to Ratcliffe, who nodded. The officer knelt and threaded the laces back through the eyes; Croft had to extend his foot like a child who cannot fasten his own shoes.

Lightfoot came to stand beside me. He was almost imperceptibly rocking backwards and forwards, as if listening to music. Tension, I supposed. 'A bad business,' he said. 'I warned you, reverend, I warned you.'

'What has he said?' I asked.

'That's not for me to tell you now, is it sir?'

I walked across the sandy soil towards Ratcliffe. The sun had become almost unbearably hot, and the only patch of greyness to be seen was a tiny cloud that touched the northern horizon. 'Harry,' I asked, 'has he told you what happened to her?'

Ratcliffe was wiping his brow with a handkerchief which he kept folded in a square. He nodded towards Croft, and as he did so drew from his pocket a pair of dark glasses.

I looked round, expecting to be prevented from talking to him, but no one appeared ready to stop me. 'Luciano?' I asked.

Croft kept looking at the ground. I was not even sure that he had heard me. Idly, like someone playing, he drew a semicircle with the toe of his shoe then remained staring at the ridge.

Ratcliffe slid his glasses onto his ears. They were too small for him, and made him look both unapproachable and quaint. 'He's been very forthcoming – haven't you, Mr Croft?'

Still Croft said nothing, but transcribed another arc with his toe.

'At the moment he's a man of few words,' Ratcliffe explained. He was amiable, even jovial. 'Thinking over what he told us before, no doubt.' Then he turned to Lightfoot. 'We're all ready, are we?'

Kim's substitute stood to one side, affecting indifference, although I could detect her unease. She was very young, no more than a girl, and could only have been with the police for a short while. But for her youth, she did not resemble Kim at all, for she was taller, more sturdily built, and blonde. Kim's clothes would never have fitted her, so she had dressed in jeans and a blouse. The zip on the jeans was pulled up an inch too short, and I could see through the thin white material of the blouse. Ratcliffe stood beside her like a master of ceremonies, his brow shining with sweat. 'Don't worry,' he reassured her, 'you'll learn a lot from this.' Then he called across to Croft. 'Lucky, we'll do this step by step. All right?'

Croft nodded.

'We're all here to help you remember, Lucky. We appreciate it was dark, so take your time and do your best.'

Croft looked up. His face looked numb and slightly swollen.

'This lady here is your daughter Kim. She'll do as you tell her. Just act out what happened last night.'

'Yes,' Croft said. He squinted up at the sun and for a moment appeared boyish. The heat was increasing, and some of the police adjusted the peaks of their caps against the glare. Apart from the one cloud the sky was a deep, clear blue, and no wind stirred.

Ratcliffe looked from face to face as if making an inventory. 'Well,' he said to Lightfoot; 'we can't wait all day, can we?'

'No sir.'

Behind me one of the men lifted a video camera onto his shoulder and began filming. Croft stepped to one side and looked askance at the lens.

Ratcliffe had the girl by the elbow and led her towards Croft. I could see her eyes react to his closeness, as if she feared him. 'You took her from Mr Fretwell's cottage during the night?'

Croft stood quiet, and I did not think he would answer, but finally he said, 'That's right.'

'You didn't have to break in?'

'No. I just turned the handle.'

157

'What did you tell her?'

'I told her to come quietly.'

'And she did?'

'She hardly spoke. We walked down the road to where I had parked the car.'

'Just there – by the gate?'

'Yes.'

'And then you took her onto the reserve?'

'She asked why, and I said I couldn't tell her. I set off and she walked behind me.'

Ratcliffe motioned for Croft to lead the way, but he held up his arm so that sunlight flared on the manacle. Ratcliffe paused a moment, then nodded to one of the policemen who had brought Croft. The handcuffs were unlocked. I expected Croft to rub his wrists, but the freed hand was left to hang limply by his side.

We began to cross the reserve. Only the leaders kept to the path; the others fanned out and were soon struggling across coarse grass and sand. I fell back behind the man with the camera, but Ratcliffe called me forward again, telling me that since I knew the dunes better than anyone I should be there to guide and advise as required. 'Between you and me,' he murmured to me 'the man's gone crazy. We need to keep an eye on him.'

'He did it, then?' I asked.

He looked at me as if, behind his dark glasses, he was startled. 'Of course he did,' he said, as if

I had asked the question out of mere intransigence or stupidity.

The patch of buckthorn funnelled us into a single file. We tramped across dozens of fresh rabbit tracks. 'You were still in front?' Ratcliffe asked.

Croft stopped and turned, his eyes dark and his face waxen. 'I didn't look back, but she stayed behind me, as if I was leading her to safety. She could have run if she'd wanted to.'

'She trusted you too much,' I said, suddenly furious with him, but Ratcliffe motioned for me to be silent.

'When we got here I held her hand. I was scared that she might stumble and hurt herself on the thorns.'

I heard someone else murmur with anger, but did not know who it was. Ratcliffe said to the girl, 'Kim, come and take your place.' She stood closer to Croft, who took hold of her bare arm. I could see her stiffen, and in Croft's eyes there was a reaction like that of mild shock. 'Maurice, how does this place look at night?'

'It's easy if you take your time,' I said. I had trodden it myself many times when it had been a ghostly path through a black thicket of thorn. I imagined them walking along it, the two of them under a starry sky, with wind making the thorn points tremble and sand whirl in dust-devils across the slopes and hillocks.

159

Suddenly the girl gave a small cry, and tried to twist her arm free. I could see how Croft's grip had strengthened so that his fingers dug into her flesh. '*Easy*,' Ratcliffe warned, and the grip relaxed while the girl stared at him with a mixture of anger and apprehension.

Within a few steps we had encountered a hot, feral smell that hung thickly in the motionless air. 'My God,' I heard someone ask behind me, 'what's that?'

'It's a fox,' I explained. 'Sometimes one comes onto the reserve at night and scavenges.' But the smell was recent, as if the fox was close by. I wondered if it had dug a hide within the thorn. If it had, it would be almost impossible to root it out.

We walked on, reached the edge of the thorn, and began to walk into a shallow depression. At its seaward side, but smudged by last night's wind, I could see indentations in the sand where something had scrambled to mount the rim. Along the far ridge the grass stalks were perfectly, unnaturally still. I looked up, expecting the gulls to be wheeling, but they were silent as if at the approach of a storm, and only a few solitary birds could be seen high in the sky. The cloud had drifted towards us and become unexpectedly large, looking darker and more ominous than I would ever have expected.

Croft took the girl in his grip again and began to scramble out of the depression, obliterating the marks that had been there. We followed him, panting and sweating, as he walked swiftly across the brow of the dune. Sand slipped and cascaded from under my feet. I was breathing heavily and my mouth was dry. I had wiped it with the back of my hand and could now feel specks of grit against my tongue. Intermittently I could smell fox, as heavily and as immediately as if the animal itself was breathing into my nostrils.

To either side of me was a ragged line of policemen, stooped and scrambling on all fours up a slope which sagged and crumbled beneath them. All was silent but for our harsh breathing and the tiny slithering rush of sand. And, although we were in full sunlight, I could see the startling blackness of the cloud spread upwards through the sky like a stain.

I called after Croft, but he ignored me as he marched towards the sea, still propelling the girl forward. I forced myself to run but was on the stones before I caught up with him. 'Lucky,' I cried, and tried to grab his arm. I could not, and merely brushed it. He glanced at me and I saw that his face was transfigured with grief. I stepped back, startled, and they continued on their way to the rock pool, the pebbles clattering as they strode.

The police pursued them, sweeping past me in a din of rattling stone. By the time I had caught them up, they were all standing round the pool and Ratcliffe was urging Croft to tell him more. 'This is where you did it, Lucky? This is where you wiped out sixteen years of your life?'

Croft was gazing at the surface of the pool, which had begun to reflect the darkness spreading over our heads. Two of the police craned over the pool and peered into it as if, like birds, they were searching for finds among the rocks.

'How long did it take?' Ratcliffe asked, and there was a triumphant ring to his voice, as if at last he was reaching the heart of his investigation.

Croft turned to the girl, who stood her ground even though I could see that she was forcing herself not to tremble. His hands reached up and he placed them on either side of her face. They stood like that for a moment, and then she pulled herself away, brushing her cheeks with her own hands as if to remove dirt.

'Not long,' Croft said. 'I kissed her and said good-bye, then I held her under. She wasn't very strong. I didn't dare look at her, so I had my eyes closed, but I could feel her hair as it floated round my wrists.'

'Lucky?' I asked, and yet was almost afraid to speak.

He looked at me with eyes that were bruised and painful.

'Lucky, was she your own child?'

He nodded gracelessly, as if it were a nervous twitch rather than assent. My legs were so weak I wanted to fall to the ground, but Lightfoot stood beside me and I could feel his hands brace me. I realised I must have swayed and looked faint.

'When she had stopped moving I still held her where she was,' Croft went on. 'I held her until my arms had gone numb up to the shoulders. Then I let her rise to the surface.'

I forced myself to look into the pool. On its floor a large crab slid beneath the black fronds of seaweed.

'Then you lifted her out?' Ratcliffe asked.

'I lifted her to me. The water streamed from her. Her skin looked like marble flecked with rain.'

'But what did you *feel*,' I heard myself ask, and was surprised at how my voice rasped with anger.

'Like a man who has done a necessary act.'

I shook my head in disbelief. 'Lucky, how could such an act be necessary?'

Croft did not answer, but stood looking at the girl who did her best to hold his gaze unblinkingly.

'Not so much a necessity as a convenience,' Ratcliffe said drily. 'You felt you had to do it to be free, didn't you?'

'The reverend knows what I mean.'

I could feel them all turn to me.

'I've no idea what you're talking about,' I said.

'What would Abraham have felt if he'd had to kill Isaac?'

CHRISTOPHER BURNS

'I think,' Ratcliffe said, with the same tone he had used the last time he had spoken, 'that we'll forget the religious overtones, if you don't mind. What did you do with your daughter once you'd picked her up?'

I reached down and touched the surface of the pool, as if in such a way I could form some kind of link with what had happened. The ripples spread slowly, as if through something more viscous than water. When I lifted my fingers the water ran down them, and I put my hand to my mouth and tasted it.

'It's fresh,' I said in wonderment.

Once more I became the centre of attention.

'There's no spring and the water's fresh,' I insisted.

Ratcliffe turned to one of his men. 'A sample might be in order. We can check what's in the girl's lungs.'

A man stepped forward. 'Will the sea have been over this since she died?'

'Yes.'

The man tasted the water himself. 'It's common seawater,' he said, shaking the excess from his hand. 'You were mistaken, reverend.'

Ratcliffe smiled humourlessly at me. 'Want to check again?'

'No,' I replied, humiliated.

'You're not too reliable, are you, Maurice?' he asked. Then, turning back to Croft, he asked again what he had done with Kim.

The edge of the cloud passed over us, blocking out the sun, making everything muted and dark. The cloud was so low that it seemed only a few feet above the crests of the dunes, and its blackness was so dense that it appeared solid. All around us visibility began to contract, and a strange sense of the unreal began to possess me. Even the sea had turned sluggish, and the waves broke with the consistency of heavy oil.

We followed Croft and the girl up the darkening beach towards the observation hut. I was near to exhaustion and stumbled twice before I reached the rise of the first dune, and had to ascend that by hauling myself upwards on marram which stung my palms. Many reached the scene before me, and stood there in a line.

In this light the flint bed looked to be made of stones the colour of jet among ground that resembled silt. At its side, just opposite the hut, the fox stood among disturbed sand. It had dug into the base of the dune and pulled something from it; a twisted rag was strewn across the ground as if it had been dragged and then let fall. Still embedded in the dune's flank was a patch of unnerving whiteness, and above that a mass of black, faintly shining material. With impossible slowness the fox turned its head and looked at us across the darkening space.

I fell onto my knees as the fox turned again and began to run up the slope of the dune in easy, loping strides. I placed my hands on the ground; beneath the palms I could feel roots, grit, fragments of shell. The silence was like a pressure in my eardrums. I retched briefly, like a dog, and a thin trail of spittle hung from my lips. Small drops of rain began to pock the sand and hit the backs of my hands. Where they fell on the sand I could see their tiny circles change the dry grit into suspensions like dark saliva. I was helpless in a strange and terrible dream.

It had become so dark that it seemed as if the world had tilted on its axis and that night was falling. Croft and the girl were a few steps towards the centre of the flint bed, and the line of police stood like a row of guardians around me. No one moved. Rain began to teem from the sky, and I could hear the infinite variety of its sounds as it struck grass, stones, clothes, caps, sand. All light had leached from the sky but the downpour held a flickering satiny luminescence.

I struggled to my feet like a man escaping quicksand, and still I was the only one to move. The ground dragged at my feet and as I walked through the grasses their edges touched me as if a scourge was being passed lightly across my skin. Ahead of me I could see the girl, motionless in the cloudburst, her clothes drenched and almost transparent. Next to her Croft tilted his head to the heavens, but his eyes were closed tightly and streams of water coursed down his face. I grabbed hold of the girl's arm; it was cold and slippery, like the limb of someone drowned. 'I can shelter you,' I said. I could taste fresh water on my tongue.

She jerked her head towards me and her sodden hair swayed heavily, but her look was uncomprehending. I tugged at her. She came away from Croft's grip quite easily, and I pulled her towards me as if I pulled her from beneath a rippling sheet of water. We collided. For a moment she was in my arms and I could feel the wetness of her body through the clothes that clung and slipped on her like a skin being shed.

'I can save you,' I shouted at her.

She spread her arms to show how wet she was. 'It's too late,' she said.

I caught hold of her again and began to climb through the sand towards the door of the hut. She did not pull away, but followed me without protest.

I was breathless when we reached the door, and had to draw lungfuls of damp air as I leaned against the sticky wood. I could hear myself wheezing as I began to search for my key. Then I saw that the door was not locked; I must have left it open when I guided Kim and Croft across the dunes. There would be a bolt inside, though; I had often fastened it when I sat inside the hut on windy days. I looked behind and saw Croft begin to climb towards us.

I pulled open the door, breaking my fingernails on it. As we struggled into the hut I trod the discarded lock into the sand. I pulled the door shut behind us and ran my hands over its inner surface to find the bolt, for the shutters were closed and we were in almost total blackness. My fingers fluttered across the grain like a blind man's until, at last, I touched metal and forced the bolt home. The girl was coughing and spluttering beside me. In the blackness I knocked against something with my leg, and found that it was the spade. I could locate it quite easily, and when I ran my hands across its cutting edge I found it coated with sand. If I had not left this door unlocked then Croft would not have been able to use it.

Dizzy, I put out my hands to touch the walls. There was a thump on the door as if someone had fallen against it, and a sharp, eerie yell. Then there was a succession, a battery of blows. I could hear a fist, and perhaps the toes of boots, against a background of hissing rain. I pressed my body against the inside of the door and could feel the force of the attack as it shivered through the wood.

For a second or two it ceased, then began again on one of the walls. I moved to the place as quickly as I could, thinking that if I wedged myself against the point of impact I could somehow absorb its energy and prevent the planks from yielding. I knocked against the girl, stumbled over her as if in a farce, and knocked a jar from the shelf. The jar bounced hollowly and rolled away across the floor. Then the hut began to tilt, and I knew that someone was trying to lever open the shutters.

The girl was leaning against me, but I could not tell if she had fallen like this or was trying to protect herself from me. She had stopped coughing and had become silent. I heard the sides of the hut creak, then groan.

I pressed myself against the shutter, pushing outward with my hands. 'Luciano,' I pleaded, 'leave me alone.' I did not beg for the girl, but only for myself.

The pressure eased, then restarted a moment later on the next shutter. 'Luciano?' I asked. My voice had become haggard and desperate, and I had begun to shake like a victim of malaria. The wood groaned. I had begun to think that this would never end, and that I was being tormented like a sufferer in a dark age hell.

The girl spoke. Her voice was calm, light, and frighteningly matter-of-fact. 'You should understand why this is happening to you, Maurice,' she said. I slid down the wooden wall because I no longer had strength to do anything but lean against it. The skin was crawling across my back and shoulders.

I peered into the aching dark; when I tried to speak my voice fractured. 'Kim?'

'Don't grieve for me,' she said, 'I knew why.'

The patterning of the downpour changed, lessened, and lifted. In the darkness I reached out for Kim. Another hand touched mine. It was small, fragile, and the fingers interlaced with my own. My arm trembled from wrist to shoulder, as if a current passed through it. I wondered if the dark would be dispelled by a light, mysterious, radiant, without a source. 'Kim,' I asked, 'is that you?'

There was no reply.

All noise had faded from outside the hut, and instead we inhabited a hushed quiet. A cold, clear light began to grow in razor-thin lines at the edges of the shutters. As it did I began to see the face of the girl who was with me; it grew imperceptibly out of the darkness as the image of a photograph surfaces from blankness. I could see that the shadows made her blonde hair the colour of ash, and how even in the gloom her eyes were not dark, but pale.

Her hand was suddenly larger and stronger than I had thought, and I took my own hand away.

'You're not her,' I said.

She stared at me with wide eyes.

'Just now – did you say anything?'

She did not move, could not speak.

'Anything at all?'

She shook her head.

I rested my body on the door as the light strengthened. My heart was lurching. Faintly, as if muffled by distance, I could hear voices begin to call my name, and another, one I did not know – the name of the girl.

I found the bolt and slid it back. It cracked sharply. Then I pushed the door. White, cold light entered the hide.

Outside everything was covered by a thin layer of pure white snow. I could smell the air; its purity was as sharp as a blade; I could hear each drip of meltwater as it ran from the hut roof, tapping in a complex pattern on the honeycombed snow at the base of the walls. The policemen were gathered round, but were moving only slowly. I could hear the air rustle in their throats, and as they dusted snow from their clothes I could see crystals drift and hang in the air, hear them crunch. Croft was being helped to his feet; I heard the sound of the policeman's fingers as they sank into the cloth of his jacket, the murmur of shoe leather and the sigh of wetness as he sought a foothold. A damp stain spread like a mark where he had fallen to his knees.

Snow lay like an opaque veil across the flint bed, making its chipped stones seem even, almost geo-metrical. The marram stalks glistened as flakes melted down them. The far dune was coated with a white, seamless drift, a creation of such flawless symmetry that it could only be perishable. Even as I watched the snow began to deliquesce. Towards the base of the dune, where the fox had dug, there was a hummock in the snow that was marked by a patch of strawberry-red stain.

I took a step forward. The snowflakes tore and sighed under my heel. The cloud above our heads parted and a shaft of sunlight touched the top of the far dune, slid like a thin brilliant searchlight down its flank, and rested momentarily on the hummock at its base before fading.

9

YESTERDAY A SQUALLY WIND BROUGHT FLURRIES of sleety rain scudding across the sea. In the afternoon I took one of the spars I had hauled up from the beach, balanced it on trestles within the shelter next to the cottage, and began to saw it into logs. After a short while I became tired, but I forced myself on until the exhaustion sank beneath the mechanics of the task, and I had a stack of logs that would last for several days standing among mounds of trodden sawdust. Occasional rain battered on the corrugated-iron roof, and sometimes the wind gusted so hard that I could see the uprights move and hear the metal as it shifted slightly, making a noise like the point of a nail dragged along a wall.

I took the logs inside and stood a few of them by the fire to dry. After I had eaten a light meal, I placed one on top of the coal and sat for a long while as the flames licked round it then caught. Once, it cracked as sharply as a pistol, and sent a shower of live sparks onto the carpet. I had to stand quickly on them to extinguish them, and for some minutes afterwards the room was full of the smell of singed wool.

When the darkness had fallen I moved my table to just beneath the light, spread a magazine on it, and flattened a blank air letter on top of that. My last letter, the first I had written to Jessica for a long time, had been condensed but confused. It had tried to re-open a dialogue with her, but at the same time it had been top-heavy with my own turmoil, distress, guilt. Almost straight away an answer had come back – urgent, concerned, and yet not fully understanding what I had been trying to say. Was I all right, Jessica asked; should she fly over to see me? Did I need any help? She could not follow what had happened that had made me write in such a way – had it been a terrible accident, or worse? Had it made me ill, or given me some kind of insight? I had sat with her reply for a long time, and finally I had slept with it beside my bed so that I could read it again as soon as I woke up.

This time I tried to be clear and informative and not to show emotion, unless its expression was carefully weighed. I began by summarising the forensic evidence, then told her about how Ratcliffe had given his version of the truth – factually, heartlessly, as if everything were linked in a secular chain of cause and effect.

I wrote in a tidy, unhurried script; the fire sparked again, but without its former ferocity.

My own evidence was completed this morning, I wrote. *After Ratcliffe, it was predictable that my own attempts to define the truth should appear difficult, partial, even contradictory. I was taken through events in miniscule detail – the 'stolen' car, the two doors left open, the request for asylum. I knew that I was portraying myself as either an accomplice or a fool, and that I would be judged the latter. None of them will see what I have begun to understand – that I was, without realising it, and in ways which I did not then recognise, an accomplice after all.*

I leaned back. A few drops of rain came down the chimney and sizzled in the fire.

I used to put my trust in institutions such as the process of law, I continued. *I recognised their limitations, but believed in their ultimate value as social and moral regulators. Now I can see that the result of Croft's trial (a foregone conclusion) will satisfy that process. But it will have little to do with what I would call Truth.*

Or what Jessica would call Truth, I thought as, later, I lay in bed and stared at the opposite wall. I had moved the crucifix back to its original position so that it faced me in the gloom. Unable to sleep for a while, I got up and returned to the letter, which I had not sealed, and wrote below my signature. *Perhaps, sometime soon, you and I will be able to discuss such things.* Then I licked the gum, sealed the letter, and placed it in the inside pocket of my coat.

Back in bed I confessed to myself that I had not been completely candid with Jessica. The years of separation had left their mark; I was not yet ready to say what the questioning had helped me understand – that I was wrong when I had thought of my part as unimportant and peripheral. Instead, I had come to realise that I was bound up with the invisible and undetected processes of fate; Croft's visit and Kim's murder had moved on me as surely as a giant weight moves on a tiny pulley.

This morning I woke to the sound of heavy, saturating rain. Clouds were massed above the reserve and trailed mist down towards the dune tops. Every stone shone like oily metal.

I ate a little, and dressed for my morning walk across the dunes, but as I was leaving by the front door Celia called. I noticed, with neither envy nor interest, that she had a new car. As soon as it halted I could see globules form on the waxing and run in narrow streams down its sleek curves. Celia said that she was just passing; it was the kind of limp excuse she often made. Both of us understood that she was concerned about me, although this was seldom directly expressed.

I did not invite her into the cottage; instead we sat in the car while raindrops pattered the roof. I wound down the window, but mist still formed on the inside of the glass, and when I ran my knuckles across the windscreen they came away wet.

'You don't look well,' she said; 'I worry about you.'

Idly, I put my fingertips to the glass again. Each mark they made was unclear, refractive. They were untrustworthy eye-slits out onto the world.

'Can I be of any help?' she asked after a while.

I shook my head, then remembered the letter. 'Yes,' I said, handing it to her, 'post this, if you don't mind. You're going straight back, aren't you?'

She placed it on the dashboard. 'I'm pleased you're writing to her. A person shouldn't let a conflict of beliefs stand between him and his family.'

'We've been apart a long time. She's almost a stranger now. That makes it easier, in some ways.'

'You're fortunate to have someone.'

I nodded. Celia wanted to tell me she had no one, but I did not wish to hear it.

'You're going to India?'

'I don't think so. Perhaps someday.'

'You would go to that ashram?'

'That's where she lives.'

'There was a time, Maurice, not too long ago, when your pride wouldn't have let you do that. You've changed.'

'That isn't a compliment, is it?'

'No.'

CHRISTOPHER BURNS

'It may not happen, Celia. I would like to see my family. Is that bad?'

'Of course not. But I suspect you would just use them as an introduction to their teacher. And who would he be? An old man who's part phoney, part deluded. Aren't people out there consciously rejecting the life of responsibility and emotional maturity? You used to think they were the enemy.'

'That was an old fool's prejudice. What is it that you find so objectionable about such religions? I don't agree with Jessica, but at least she believes in a divine intervention in the affairs of men, at least she tries to understand *resonance*. They see it too softly, too selfishly, that's all.'

After a pause, Celia replied in measured tones. 'I find such ideas both offensive and ludicrous.'

I shrugged. I no longer had any missionary zeal, and was indifferent to her disapproval. 'I must go,' I said, and put my hand on the door handle.

'A minute more, Maurice. Please.'

I settled back into the passenger seat. She leaned towards me and tried to fix me with her gaze. I could tell that she was trying to be honest and to speak without compromise, but I felt like a teacher being lectured by a didactic child. 'Maurice, why did you let yourself be treated like that at the trial? You were no match for those questions, and yet you used to be fluent, confident, able to win your way by the power of argument. Instead you offered yourself up for sacrifice. You were stumbling, absurdly metaphysical, unworldly. You even said that only God would know the truth, and yet he chose to hide it from us. Don't you see that's precisely what a trial is for? And don't tell me about the failures of the judicial system, I know all about them. This trial is straightforward, with no doubt about what happened.'

'Or why?'

She made a small, exasperated sound. 'It doesn't take a genius to see that Luciano Croft had covered up so much in his life that he finally cracked. The girl didn't even know she was his daughter. Neither did his wife when she was alive.'

I said nothing. I had wondered if Kim knew. She had wanted to settle down, not among refugees, but among Americans. Perhaps she was just waiting for her father to admit the truth.

'It all got too much for him, that's all. He broke apart, and afterwards didn't know how to react. It wasn't a cold-blooded crime, whatever Ratcliffe might think; it was a crime of despair, of agony. He's not evil and he's not a villain. If there are villains in this piece, it's the Thucs. They're the ones who still refuse to admit they're the girl's relatives.'

'As you say, they still deny it. Perhaps they're right. The evidence was flimsy.'

'It was enough for me,' she replied.

'You once told me that only lawyers worried about facts; reporters looked for connections. *It's the pattern that matters*, you said.'

Her mouth twisted in annoyance. 'The Thucs must be covering up far more than Luciano Croft ever did. All right, it may be about their sister, it may be about themselves – who knows what they did before the city fell? But by their refusal to acknowledge her, they condemned Kim to death.'

'They weren't to know that.'

'No, but they must have had *some* idea of the consequences of their actions.'

'My testimony was true, Celia. God hides the truth from us.'

'God?' she asked, and I saw a momentary sneer cross her face. 'What happened to you, Maurice?'

'I'm a different person,' I said simply.

'You talk about truth, and yet you used to say that we had to find truth in the raw material of human existence. You argued that mankind must give itself shape and direction by the application of a humanist morality based on Christian precepts. And now you talk to me about God!'

'The truth,' I said patiently, 'is that Luciano Croft drowned his daughter in the rock pool. All this was prefigured in my own life. I did not respond to the Edmondson girl's death, and now I have Kim's murder.'

'Why do you interpret everything in terms of yourself?'

I sat and looked at the condensation run down the window.

'Maurice, isn't that the most selfish approach you could take? And don't you think that the remorse and distress caused to the Edmondsons, and maybe to Croft as well, will be infinitely greater than whatever you feel?'

'Probably that's true.'

She was exasperated, and refused to follow me. 'Well then?'

'I can only interpret events as they affect me, Celia. God weaves subtly dark patterns, labyrinthine ones; I can only just see the one that is being woven for me, and I cannot know what is being woven for you. There are so many ways in which I could have acted differently. It was not just that I was a holy fool, an innocent abroad in a treacherous world; by my actions, I denied God's purpose until I had to confront it.'

'You're talking nonsense. Of course you didn't.'

'You're wrong. I was given the Edmondson tragedy – do you realise that? I was given it as a test.'

'By your precious God, I suppose. I wouldn't want anything to do with such a God.'

'For a long time, neither did I. God put me to the test, with the Crofts, too. He gave me that because I'd failed all the others.'

'This is madness, Maurice. You're too intelligent to believe there's a kind of divine game going on in which individuals benefit because of the sufferings of innocents. How could you reach such a conclusion – you of all people?'

'I must do. How many young girls would have had to die before I came to my senses? I tasted the water, Celia. It was fresh. But I allowed myself to be persuaded otherwise.'

'It was salt in her lungs.'

'You miss the point. And I heard her voice, as clear and as close to me as yours is now. I sat beside her in the hut, I *touched* her. When I opened the door there was snow, like the snow that used to fall in midsummer for the saints, and a finger of light from heaven pointing to where the body lay. Some reach God by force of intellect, Celia, and some by the power of faith. I had his existence proved to me. I was the kind who needed evidence, and I was given it. I'm a chosen man. I never thought I would be, but I am, and now everything has changed and it can never change back. Never.'

'I was at the gate, remember? We all saw the storm coming. It was unusual, but not unique; there have been patches of bizarre weather since records began. That tiny blizzard even made the television that night. It edged down the coast for twenty miles or so before it exhausted itself. There were jokes about it in the newspapers the very next day. No one but you saw it as anything but irritatingly odd. The police even tried to get in the hide with you, just for shelter, but you'd bolted the door. I think Ratcliffe was scared *you*'d gone crazy, too. And as for voices – did anyone else hear one? The girl who was with you remembers nothing apart from some strange behaviour from you.'

I did not answer.

'You'd been ill, Maurice. You collapsed just a day or so before the re-enactment, didn't you? Small wonder you weren't quite functioning normally. And as for fingers of light – well, you've seen clouds part over the dunes more times than most of us. Did you ever before see something like that? Because, when you did, you would have seen them as perfectly ordinary aspects of meteorology.'

'When Saul was on his way to Damascus, did his companions see what he saw, hear what he heard? Your arguments are useless, Celia. Now let me go.'

I got out of the car and stood in the rain, pulling my collar up around my neck. Celia wound down the window. Her eyes were bright with either sadness or anger, I could not tell which. 'You had an integrity about you once, Maurice. It made you uncomfortable to be with, but you were worthy. What have you traded your honour for? A belief in an Old Testament God? It's a shallow and complacent belief. You used to be too good for that.'

'Complacent?' The word had not occurred to me. 'I'm not complacent, Celia. How could anyone be complacent when they know they are being judged?'

I walked towards the gate. Water was sluicing down the road and the rain was hitting in large white splashes. I heard the car door open behind me.

'At least Lucky Croft's judge is real,' Celia called. 'At least he's accountable, his judgement is subject to appeal, and it's even possible that the populace expresses the general will through him. He's not a figment of the imagination, a leftover from the days of barbarism and superstition, a bitter and lunatic anachronism.'

I closed the gate behind me. The latch crashed home. Grass squelched under my boots, and I felt the sand shift as I trod on it.

After I had gone a dozen steps she called again, but her voice was as misty as the rain. 'Maurice,' she cried, 'despite everything, I still believe in human goodness.'

I walked on, crossing the drenched hummocks and heading directly to the beach. Cloud was unbroken across the sea, although at the horizon there was a yellowish line, like a stain. The tide was coming in fast, sweeping across the ribbed sand in thin waves. At its wash bubbles broke among tiny rafts of foam.

I walked through the downpour along the strand until I reached the rock pool. Rain pocked its surface like the marks of a disease. I pushed up the sleeves of my coat, stooped, and placed my hands in the water. Seaweed brushed my wrists and a crab moved across the floor in a crippled glide. After my hands had become numb I took them out and licked one wrist experimentally. The water was salty.

As I stood there, a higher wave breached the far end of the pool and a ripple of froth swelled across its surface in a widening arc.

I tramped up the beach, crunching wet sand and pebbles. Although I kept my eyes on the ground, I saw only the triangular imprints of birds. By the time I reached the flint bed I was breathing laboriously and there was a pain across my chest and my head felt light. I wondered if I stood again at the edge of vision.

I walked to the very centre of the bed and dropped to my knees. A sharp stone cut into me, but I did not move, and I could feel wetness soaking through my clothes. Rain poured out of the skies; it ran down my face, dripped from my fingertips, it struck sand and pebble and broken stone. High above, as if indifferent to the earth, white gulls sailed against the darkness.

CHRISTOPHER BURNS
ABOUT THE BODY

'An uncommonly good first collection of short stories'
Robert Nye in The Guardian

'Nearly every story has some valedictory touch, some neat shift in perspective that lifts it onto a higher level of engagement . . . This is a peach of a collection'
D. J. Taylor in The Independent

'Carefully crafted, sinister little gems'
Judy Cooke in The Listener

Forthcoming from Sceptre

CHRISTOPHER BURNS
THE CONDITION OF ICE

'Put Burns's imagination on a perpendicular cliff of stratified black rock with the cracks filling with snow, and he'll have you feeling for a toe-hold in the carpet'
Independent on Sunday

'THE CONDITION OF ICE is that rare thing: a novel of action and emotion which is also a novel about the way people think. The uncertainties of its inner landscapes are pitilessly exposed, but never without sympathy . . . a tremendous achievement'
D. J. Taylor in The Independent

'Haunting . . . moving but unsentimental'
The Sunday Times

sceptre